H. Austin

The stigmata

A history of various cases

H. Austin

The stigmata
A history of various cases

ISBN/EAN: 9783741195716

Manufactured in Europe, USA, Canada, Australia, Japa

Cover: Foto ©Andreas Hilbeck / pixelio.de

Manufactured and distributed by brebook publishing software
(www.brebook.com)

H. Austin

The stigmata

THE STIGMATA:

A

HISTORY OF VARIOUS CASES.

TRANSLATED FROM

"The Mystik" of Görres.

Edited, with a Preface, by

THE REV. H. AUSTIN.

"For I bear the marks of the Lord
Jesus in my body."—*Gal.* vi. 17.

London:
THOMAS RICHARDSON AND SON,
23, King Edward Street, City;
and Derby.
1883.

PREFACE.

THE wonderful grace of the Stigmata was a thing unknown in the Church before the time of S. Francis of Assisi. It is possible there may have been unnoticed cases of partial stigmatization, but there are none on record. When S. Paul says that he bears in his body the marks (stigmata) of the Lord Jesus, he is not supposed to mean that he had impressed on his body the Five Sacred Wounds : but he alludes rather to the chains, stripes, etc., which he had borne for Christ, the marks of which were on his body. The Stigmata, properly so-called, were reserved in God's treasure-house, in a secret casket, till the day S. Francis should come to be adorned with them.

Since the day of S. Francis the Stigmata have become a not unusual grace. For, besides the most remarkable authentic cases, a multitude of others have existed, and still exist, though not publicly known, or not known to a wide circle. But this grace has its principal field of action in the family of S. Francis. The features of the father pass on in every age to his children. The gift is found to spread outside his family, but not abundantly. Its rich profusion still remains as the heritage of the children of that Saint who first received the grace.

The Stigmata are received first in the soul by an intense sympathy with our Lord in His Passion. But as the soul and body form one man, these Stigmata always aim at passing from the soul to the body, so that the body shall participate, after her manner, in that which so deeply affects the soul.

The Stigmata do not always pass from

the soul to the body. The bodies of some persons are less plastic than those of others. They less readily, and only sluggishly, conform themselves to the sentiments and affections of the soul. Thus it may well be that a person not stigmatized feels sympathy with our Lord in His Passion more intensely than another who wears the Stigmata in the body. In the latter case the body is more plastic, and is so impressionable as to reflect on the outer envelope of the body the inner workings of the soul. Again, many cases are recorded where the Stigmata without were withdrawn by our Lord, though the soul within suffered no detriment of devotion to, or of sympathy with, our Lord's Passion.

Still the wearing of our Lord's Stigmata in the body is a great grace. We shall admire in heaven those who circle round our Lord, bearing their living resemblance to Him in their bodies, being living pictures of Him in their five wounds. So on earth, when we see, or hear, or read of these wonderful effects of the love of our Lord, and of that close union of His chosen ones with Him, our hearts are naturally quickened to a deeper and more intense love of His Passion. May the reading of this little book contribute its part to make Jesus Christ crucified more loved and more adored.

CONTENTS.

CHAPTER I.

CHAPTER II.

CHAPTER III.

CHAPTER IV.

CHAPTER V.

CHAPTER VI.

The Stigmata.

—

CHAPTER I.

The Ecstatic State considered as developed in the inferior regions of life—the transformation it effects upon the body.

THE STIGMATA IN ITS TWO FIRST DEGREES: THE CROWN
OF THORNS AND THE WOUND IN THE SIDE—PREVIOUS
PREPARATION—THE CHALICE AND THE BLOODY SWEAT
— VERONICA GIULIANI—CATHARINE OF RACONISIO—
SAINT LUTGARD—THE CROWN OF THORNS ALONE—
VERONICA GIULIANI—TWO CROWNS ARE PRESENTED
TO THE ECSTATICA FOR HER CHOICE—CATHARINE OF
RACONISIO—CHRISTINA OF STUMBELEN—URSULA AGUIR
—THE WOUND IN THE SIDE — VERONICA GIULIANI—
JANE MARY OF THE CROSS—CECILIA DE NOBILI—MAR-
TINA OF AVILLA—MARY VILLANA—ANGELA OF PEACE.

MAN was created to the image and likeness of God. He was created by the
Father, in the Son, whom the Holy
Ghost unites to the Father by the bond of
love. Now, just as the Father radiates
forth eternally within Himself, in the Son,
through the Holy Ghost, so in like manner does He produce without, in time,

1

through the Son and in the Son, all creatures, including man. The whole universe shows this triple imprint. It is impressed upon the heavenly spirits no less than upon the powers and elements of the inferior creation. The image of God prevails in the former, whilst the latter resemble Him merely by likeness. On man, however, being composed of two natures, is impressed both the image and the likeness of the Divinity.

But a portion of the heavenly spirits, abusing the gift of free-will which God has bestowed upon them, turned aside their gaze from Him in whose image they had been created, and dwelt complacently upon the view of their own excellences. Thus they first of all disfigured in themselves the image of the Creator, and their fall was succeeded by a corresponding counter-shock which much impaired the likeness to the Divinity in exterior nature. Man did not escape uninjured from the general loss. The sin into which he fell resulted in obscuring the image of God in his soul, and by a necessary consequence the divine likeness which existed in his body was disfigured also.

Now man, in the order of creation, holds an

intermediate place. He stands as the connecting link between two fallen worlds,—the world of spirits and the world of exterior nature. Thus the faculties of his soul and body partake of their deterioration. The image of God being once disturbed in his soul, the creature in whom he trusted in preference to his Creator set its own seal there in the place of the stamp of God. His body also was affected by exterior nature, convulsed as it had been by the rebel angels; and rude, discordant utterances battled in the very centre of his being.

Two different effects were at once produced in him. One is the effect of the fall, whereby fallen man, linked as he is with the powers of darkness, may render this connection closer still. He can still more completely efface what remains of the divine image in him, and engrave in its stead the image of the devil, by transforming himself, as it were, into the spirit of evil. Side by side, however, with this depressing tendency sprang a contrary motion, which has become much more marked since the redemption. Its object is to reconcile man's body and soul, that is, to unite the image and likeness of God in him; to de-

stroy all that could defile either, or set them
at variance; and further, to re-establish the
divine impress, that so man may once more
become a faithful mirror of the Blessed Trinity.

This work of restoration, which was begun
in baptism, is carried on by means of a Christian life, to which the sacraments add their
sanctifying virtue. Christian asceticism leads
to a crisis, and the transforming process which
is to regenerate fallen humanity culminates
in the ecstatic state. Three things, however,
having been lost at the fall, which must
necessarily be recovered again, it is not surprising to find that ecstasy comprises three
distinct degrees, or successive stages, which
may be thus briefly described.

Under the special influence and moulding
of the Son, who has saved us by His death,
and who is the beginning of all things, being
the Way, the Truth, and the Life, the lower
life in man is first transformed and restored
to the divine likeness. Next, the Holy Spirit,
who, as sovereign mover of the universe,
developes every work once begun, re-estab-
lishes harmony between the image of God
which is in the spirit, and His likeness which
resides in the body. And finally, beneath

the directing hand of the Father, who is the supreme end and perfection of all things, man's new birth is completed, and the image of God is fully restored in him in all its magnificence and glory.

In the spiritual life, however, the purgative must precede both the illuminative and the unitive way. Hence it is a fundamental law of all mystic theology, that none can ascend the mount of transfiguration with our Lord without having first accompanied Him to the crucifixion on Calvary. For it is evident that genuine and effective charity must be deeply rooted in a man ere he can participate in our Saviour's Passion by means of the lively sentiments of compassion which it excites. It is only when thus prepared that he can receive from the hand of Christ, thankfully, and as a free gift on His part, the transfiguration which He acquired for him by His sufferings.

The image, therefore, into which the creature first finds itself transformed is not that of Jesus Christ glorified, but it is that of Jesus Christ suffering. The work of redemption, after having encountered pain in every shape, terminated in the death of the cross ; and our Lord's return to a higher sphere was brought about by His resurrection, which vanquished death, and by His following ascension.

Now we find the same order to be observed with regard to the work of restoration in the ecstatic state. First, the old man must completely die out under the influence of that tender compassion which associates it to the sufferings of our Lord. Thus sin and death are entirely overcome. Next, if the image of Jesus glorified be to arise in the mystical man, all the obscurity left by sin must be purged away by an imitation of Christ's death, after which he may hope to ascend from the depths of the grave to the dazzling heights of the transfiguration.

Having reached this state, man, bearing all the signs of his dying Saviour, and marked on his own body with the wounds of the Crucified, returns, as it were, with Jesus to the gates of death. There his entire being is renewed in pain and anguish before he arises glorified, to recover by degrees a perfect impression of the divine image.

This phenomenon, of which we are now about to treat, is commonly called the Stigmata.

Now the Stigmata, that complete and profound transformation of the lower life in man, does not in general appear instantaneously with its various phenomena. On the contrary, it spreads slowly and gradually over the diverse regions of life, and only consummates its work after having submitted them one and all to its own action. Neither is it usually produced unexpectedly, as though originated by a flash of lightning, but the several degrees are almost always preceded by tokens of different kinds.

It is to the study of such signs and degrees that we would devote the following pages.

In the year of our Lord 1693, Veronica Giuliani, being then thirty-three years of age, began **Veronica Giuliani.** to prepare herself to live thenceforth entirely in her Lord, that so His divine life might arise in her. Whereupon God was pleased to show her a mysterious chalice, which she at once recognized as betokening the sufferings of the Passion, which she should embrace later on. The same vision was manifested to her under different forms during those years which succeeded the first apparition. Sometimes the chalice appeared to her as a bright and splendid one; upon other

occasions, on the contrary, it was plain and
unadorned. At one time the liquid it contained seemed to be boiling, and overflowed
in great quantities. At another time it would
be falling slowly, drop by drop. She was
always willing in spirit to drain the cup thus
offered her to the very dregs, but the flesh
recoiled with horror from the thought of it.
Finally, however, the spirit won the mastery,
and with a deep sigh she said : " Lord, when
wilt Thou give me this chalice ? I thirst,
I thirst, not for consolations, but for bitterness and sufferings." At length one night,
when she was engaged in prayer, our Lord
yielded to her entreaties, and, appearing to her
with the chalice, He spoke thus; "Whether
thou shouldst take this and taste of it depends
upon thyself, but the hour is not yet come.
Prepare to receive it at the appointed time."
After this the Blessed Virgin came to her
several times and encouraged her.

Upon another occasion our Lord showed
Himself to her, bound to the pillar, His body
all covered with wounds, and drenched with
blood. · He bore the chalice in His hands
as before, and thus addressed her: "Behold
these Wounds, My beloved; hearken to the

voice of their cry. They plead with thee to
drink of the same bitter chalice which I Myself once drained. Lo, I give it to thee.
That thou shouldst taste it is My will." He
then vanished from her sight, but the chalice
remained. She felt strengthened both in
body and soul, and her heart was inflamed
with desire to obey the will of God. Nevertheless nature still shrank from the chalice,
and the struggle produced a violent fever,
which took entire possession of her. Sometimes she beheld the cup poured out upon
her, and she would then feel herself devoured
by a consuming fire, which increased her thirst
the more she tried to assuage it by drinking.
Again she would see one drop fall from the
chalice upon what she chanced to be eating,
and her palate would for a long while after
retain such a taste of bitterness and gall as to
cause her much suffering. If she looked at
the drops they seemed to change into swords
and lances, which pierced her heart through
and through. Nor was this the whole of what
she had to endure. She was obliged, in
obedience to her superiors, to submit to a
course of treatment prescribed by certain
physicians, which merely served to increase

her sufferings. And in addition to all this she was forced to combat many temptations, and she was tormented by an interior dryness of spirit so terrible that it seemed to her as though the very agony of death could not exceed it.

All these details, which were furnished by herself, have been collected together in her life, which was drawn up from well-authenticated documents, by M. Salvatori, a priest, at Rome, in 1803. (See p. 60.)

Catharine of Raconisio. Another chalice, the harbinger betokening a similar state, was presented to Catharine of Raconisio. She was born in that part of Piedmont so named, in the year 1486. When she was four years old, as she was gazing at an image which represented the martyrdom of Saint Peter, she was seized with a most vehement desire of imitating him. The holy apostle at once offered her a chalice, saying: "My daughter, take and drink the Blood of Him who redeemed thee, that so, strengthened by Him, thou mayest be able to drink likewise of the chalice of His most bitter Passion." Scarcely had she drunk a few drops than she became as though inebriated with the love of God. She was so completely overcome that she could not stand upright, but was fain to lean for support against the walls of the church.

Hence we find that as our Lord's Passion, which prefigures that of His saints, began in the Garden of Olives, so these His followers have to enter upon their path of suffering on the same spot, and those who would follow so closely in His track must drink of the chalice which was presented to Him there. We are thus led to infer that the Bloody Sweat which fell from His sacred Body in the garden would be reproduced in the mystical Passion which they undergo; and so it proves, for this portion of His agony continually recurs in the opening scene which seems to serve as a prelude to all that succeeds it.

Many instances of this kind might be quoted. One, however, will suffice, that of Saint Lutgard. **Saint Lutgard.** Of her we are told that she was often rapt in ecstasy when she meditated upon our Lord's Passion. Her body then became bathed in bloody sweat, which all might behold, flowing down from her face and hands. (Henriquez de B. Lutgard, June 16.)

Sometimes a cross is manifested as well as the chalice. This was the case with Catharine of Raconisio. Our Lord twice placed His cross upon her shoulders to try her, and as upon the second occasion she accepted it with resignation, one of her shoulders remained during her whole life burdened as with a heavy weight. It was lower than the other, and she experienced certain pains in it which augmented one by one. (See her Life, written by Razzi, compiled from Pie de la Mirandola's MSS. It was inserted by Marchese, in the Diario Dominicano, t. 1, Sept.)

Generally speaking, the bestowal of the Stigmata, properly so called, commences with the presentation of the Crown of Thorns, and the attendant circumstances are always much the same. Veronica Giuliani herself relates what took place in this respect when the chalice of the Passion was offered to her. She writes thus : "On the night of the 4th of April, 1694, when I was deeply absorbed in prayer, I had a vision of our Blessed Lord, who appeared to me, wearing a crown of thorns. On seeing this I exclaimed, 'Give me those thorns, my Beloved, for mine they

should be, not Thine, O my Sovereign Good!'
Then I heard Him answer me, saying, 'Verily
am I come to crown My beloved one.' And
thus speaking, He took the crown of thorns
from off His own Head, and placed it upon
mine. The pain I that instant experienced
was so intense that I never remember to have
suffered any greater. When I recovered
myself the pain still continued, so that I was
unable to stand, and I felt my strength failing
me. Therefore I besought the Lord to give
me sufficient strength to fulfil the duties of
my charge in the convent, and to enable me
to conceal from others the graces He should
deign to bestow upon me. I instantly regained my strength, and was thus able to
attend to my ordinary occupations, but I continued to feel the pain caused by the thorns,
and each time I inclined my head I thought I
must have died. And after this, whenever
during prayer the desire of suffering was
renewed in me, I could feel the thorns penetrating more deeply into my head, so that
often the pain overpowered me, and I remained a long while unconscious. But all
that I underwent merely served to increase
the desire of suffering in my heart, and such

desire was invariably succeeded by fresh suffering, so that it seemed as though one pain brought on another."

This state of things lasted all the remainder of her life, that is to say, for thirty-four or thirty-five years, and, judging from what she wrote down during the first twelve years after her painful coronation, it would seem that throughout that period the violence of the pains was intermittent, but she was never free from them. On Fridays and on fast days they augmented, and in Holy Week they became intolerable. At such times she was accustomed to turn to God, and to say, " Lord, if it be Thou who art pressing down these thorns, force them in deeper still, that so I may suffer more."

Her sufferings at length came to the knowledge of her superiors, and Sister Florida Ceoli was appointed to examine her head. She accordingly did so, and afterwards affirmed the following statement upon oath :

" The head was surrounded by a red ring, which was at times set with small projections about the size of a pin's head. At other times the ring was encircled with violet marks, thorn-like in shape, which descended towards

the eyes; one even struck down far enough
to be visible underneath the right eye. Some
tears dropped from that eye, which, when
gathered up upon a cloth, were found to be
mingled with blood."

The bishop, Ant. Eustochi, was not content
with Sister Florida's report alone, but determined to send certain physicians and surgeons,
who should ascertain the state of the case.
They undertook to cure the sufferer, thereby
affording her an opportunity of acquiring
greater merit. They first proceeded to bathe
the head with a certain kind of oil, which produced such intense heat that she thought her
skull to be on fire, although she at the same
time experienced an icy coldness within the
brain. They then determined to apply moxas
upon her head and upon one foot. The courage she manifested upon this occasion filled
all about her with admiration. Not one of
the Sisters could endure the spectacle of the
suffering she underwent; but she, meanwhile,
herself encouraged the surgeon, Massana, and
so placid was the expression of her countenance that he might have been supposed
to be operating upon marble.

After a few days, the wound made by the

moxa upon her head closed up, and the pain became intolerable. They then applied another to her neck, but this experiment had to be given up, for the patient was thrown into such a state of nervous agitation that she had not a moment's rest either by night or by day.

The physicians now resolved to try the effect of a seton, but the nuns utterly refused to take part in a fresh operation. Veronica therefore undertook to assist the operators herself, and although this was much more painful than the preceding operation had been, she endured it with equal courage and fortitude. The sensation of cold disappeared, but the state of her head remained the same. Blisters were then set upon both her arms, but this brought on so severe an attack of cramp in her arms and feet, to add to all her other sufferings, that they were allowed to dry up. As a last attempt plasters were placed behind her ears, and then at length, every remedy having proved ineffectual, and finding that the infirmities they were trying to heal augmented instead of decreasing, the medical men yielded the point, and pronounced the Saint to be in a wholly supernatural condition, which they were powerless to relieve in any way. (See her Life. B. ii. ch. ii.)

In most cases, however, two crowns are presented to persons in ecstasy, the one being formed of flowers, or of some precious **Catharine of Raconisio.** metal, and the other of thorns, that so a free choice may be made of either. It was in this manner that our Lord appeared to Blessed Catharine of Raconisio when she was but ten years old. She chose the crown of thorns, thereby more closely to resemble her Beloved. He responded to her with a smile, saying, "Truly do I admire the generosity of thy choice; nevertheless thou art as yet merely a feeble child, and thy heart's desires exceed thy bodily strength. Not now will I crown thy brows with so painful a diadem. I reserve it for a later day."

Our Lord fulfilled His promise, for she did afterwards receive it; and Pie de la Mirandola, who himself beheld it when he was in the town where she dwelt, describes it in these words: "A circular mark surrounded her skull, formed by an indentation, which was wide and deep enough to admit a child's little finger. Around this circle there were what

2

seemed to be swellings wherein blood had settled. She told me that they bled frequently and abundantly. I myself often saw her suffer most acute pain caused by this crown, and her eyes used to become suffused with blood." (Marchese, c. iv.)

Christina of Stumbelen. Christina of Stumbelen was one of those who also received the crown of thorns, and, like Catharine of Raconisio, in her case it seems to have penetrated to the actual bone of the skull.

Peter of Dacia relates, in his life of her, that she obtained her crown eight days before Holy Week, and he adds that he himself often saw the blood flowing down from her head, beneath her veil. Sometimes it trickled in three streams over her face, each stream being about three inches wide. (A. S. June 22.)

After her death her body was carried to Nideck, whence it was transferred to Juliers in 1583, where it was laid in a tomb prepared for it there. A sort of crown, about half an inch wide, may be seen upon her skull, which is preserved at Nideck. It extends from the occiput to the forehead, widening gradually so as almost to touch the ears. It is of a greenish hue, and is sprinkled over with red points, resembling the points of thorns. Thus Steinfinder and Lulle saw it, as they declare in their writings upon the subject. (See the Acts of the Saint. L. v. 63.)

Our Lord set a crown of thorns upon the head of Ursula Aguir like- **Ursula Aguir.** wise, of the Third Order of Saint Dominic, at the same time foretelling her that she would have much to suffer. She died in 1608. (Steill. Sept. 8.)

Steph. Quinzani de Soncino, who was born in 1457, experienced the pain of the bloody sweat and the crowning with thorns on Fridays. The crown of thorns was often visible to others upon her head. (Ibid. Jan. 2.) Jane Mary of the Cross, a Poor Clare at Roveredo, who died in 1673, had the crown of thorns, but she concealed it beneath her veil. (Ibid. March.) It was also given to Mary Razzi de Chios, born in 1552; to Mary Villana, who died in 1670; to Sister Vincent Ferrer, of Valentia, who died in 1515; and to Sister Philip of St. Thomas, etc., etc. (Ibid. v. i. p. 10, 49, 515; v. ii. p. 567.) In some cases the pain of the coronation is felt, but no exterior or visible trace of it appears. Sister

Cath. Cialina, of the Third Order of Saint Francis, (about 1619,) in Italy, and Sister Emily Bicchieri de Verceil, are instances of this. (Menolog. Francisc. 472; Steill. ii. 24.)

Upon one occasion only a portion of the crown of thorns was imprinted upon the head. This was the case with Rita de Cassia, an Augustinian nun. One day, as she was considering our Lord's Passion at the foot of her crucifix, she conceived an ardent desire of participating in some of His sufferings. Whilst her mind was thus occupied she beheld one of the sharpest of the thorns detach itself from those which formed the crown upon the head of the figure representing our Lord upon the cross, before which she was, and, advancing towards her, it inflicted a deep wound in the centre of her forehead. She bore the pain occasioned by this wound with great patience to the day of her death, although it caused her much suffering, and the scar may still be seen upon her body, which is preserved intact. (See Torellus, History of Augustinian Order, A.D. 1430.)

We find the wound in the side often appearing simultaneously with the sweat of blood and the crown of thorns. And with relation to this we will once more quote from a document written by Saint Veronica Giuliani, at the command of her confessor. She had, as it appears, embraced every exercise of devotion with redoubled fervour during the winter of the year 1696, and the fire of divine love burned with renewed force in her soul. She had been appointed to call the sisters of her convent for matins, and in thus fulfilling her office she exclaimed, " See you not that daybreak is at hand, O my sisters? This is no time for sleep. Up! up! arise!" Our Lord then appeared to her in the form of a beautiful Child of most winning aspect. " He bore," she continues, " in His hand a golden sceptre. The top was surmounted with a burning flame, the other end terminated in the shape of a lance. The Child Jesus touched my head with the summit of the sceptre, and set the point of the lance upon my breast, which was instantly, as I felt, transpierced. All at once I perceived His hand empty. He looked on me tenderly, and made me understand that henceforth I was united to Him in a very intimate way. Then I both learnt and saw many things, of which, however, I do not speak, for I retain but a confused recollection of them. When I came to myself I fancied I must be mad, and I knew not what had befallen me. I felt there was an open wound over my heart, but I did not venture to look at it. I applied a handkerchief, and withdrew it, stained with blood, and I experienced great pain. Afterwards, when you had commanded me to examine the wound, to ascertain whether it were real, I did so, and I found it to be open. The opening was about as wide as the back of a large knife. It was not then bleeding, however, and the surrounding flesh seemed perfectly whole. This is what happened to me. Eight days later, on New Year's Day, the wound began to bleed again, and it remained open a long time. May all things be to the glory of God." (Her Life, p. 98.)

Jane Mary of the Cross. These wounds are not mere superficial ones. They penetrate to the heart itself. Thus Jane Mary of the Cross, at Roveredo, bore the same wound in her side, and it continued to bleed, and remained red, like the others, even after her death. When her body was examined it was found to have reached her heart.

Cecilia de Nobili, a Poor Clare, at
Nuceria in Umbria, who lived about
the year 1655, suffered during her
last illness very violent pains in her
heart. She died at the age of twenty-five.
Her body was examined after death, and a
triangular wound was discovered in her heart.
It was opposite the breast, and would appear
to have been inflicted by a lance. It narrowed
in entering the organ. (Huber. March, p.
766, and July, p. 1454.) The same thing
befel Martina d'Arilla, at Benvenuto, as she
had predicted to her confessor.

Persons in ecstasy do not, however, always
receive wounds of this kind by means of a
lance or an arrow. Gabrielle de Piezolo, at
Aquila, saw our Lord appear to her with the
wound in His side bleeding. While she was
embracing it with tender compassion, her
own side opened and bled unceasingly until
her death. (Ibid. June, p. 1257.) Sometimes
a seraph appears, instead of our Lord. Mary
of Sarmiento was wounded by a seraph. The
heart of Saint Teresa was pierced by a seraph
with a burning arrow. Traces of the wound
remain in it to this day. Margaret Columna
is another instance. Her right side was

Cecilia de Nobili.

opened, and it bled continually ever after. Mary Villana, daughter of the Margrave de Pella, was likewise wounded by an arrow. She also had the ecstatic bleeding. And Clare de Bugni, of the Third Order of S. Dominic, when she was once meditating upon the Passion, in or about the year 1514, felt her side open, and fragrant blood often issued from the wound. (Steill. i. p. 515 and 1802.)

Angela of Peace. Sister Angela of Peace, happening one day to contemplate a certain representation of S. Laurence, it came to pass that the sight of the flames which encompassed the holy martyr kindled anew in her the fire of divine love. While she was absorbed in the thought of our Blessed Lord, it pleased Him to manifest Himself to her in the form of a child. He touched her with His finger on the breast, and she felt as though she had been struck by lightning. Her heart had been transpierced. The wound as yet shed no blood, but a burning heat issued from her breast, which utterly consumed her. It seemed to her as though everything around her were on fire,—not only her garments, her bed, and the very ground on which she trod, but even cold water like-

wise. Inundated with torrents of sweat, she
vainly sought for refreshment of any kind,
and she might well have cried with the spouse
in the Canticles, "Thy love is strong as
death." But nothing could satiate her desire of love. The more it increased in her
heart, the more vehement became her longing
after it, until at length God bestowed upon
her the actual wound for which she yearned.

This favour was granted her on Holy
Thursday, in the year 1634, when she was
twenty-four years old. She was engaged in
meditating upon our Lord's Passion in her
cell, and when in due course her thoughts
rested upon the remembrance of the lance
thrust which pierced His most Sacred Heart,
her own heart was smitten with such tender
compassion that it seemed as though it would
break.

The Child Jesus then appeared to her, and
opening His breast, He discovered to her His
pierced Heart. Such intense grief overwhelmed her at the sight that she nearly died.
Having, however, somewhat overcome the
extreme anguish which the first impression
had wrought in her, she exclaimed, in a very
transport of divine love, "Pierce, O my God,

pierce my heart as deeply as once Thine own was pierced by me." Instantly she felt her right *hand* (sic) pierced by a lance. She was cast to the ground by the intensity of the pain, and she remained in a deathlike condition for three days.

The wound was open, and it bled so violently that sheer exhaustion compelled her to keep her bed for a month. Indeed, her confessor, Cornelio, entertained fears for her life. The blood which fell was thick and of so deep a hue, that even after several immersions in fresh water it was scarcely possible to wash it out of the wool which it had dyed. A certain kind of water issued as well as blood from the wound. Its likeness, however, to ordinary water consisted merely in its fluidity. It seemed to be boiling, for if a drop chanced to fall upon her hand, it not only scalded her, but it raised a blister. This wound remained open for several years, but the loss of blood was so great that finally Father Cornelio, fearing she would be completely exhausted, solemnly commanded her, in virtue of obedience, to close it. It closed at once, but re-opened at Cornelio's death, and began to bleed again, only, however, on Fridays and

on festivals, and then less profusely than
before. It was again closed by her next confessor, but she bore the scar, which was
plainly visible, until her death. (Marchese,
p. 525.)

CHAPTER II.

Of the Complete Stigmata.

THE STIGMATA APPEARS FOR THE FIRST TIME UPON S.
FRANCIS OF ASSISI—THE SYMPTOMS WHICH PRECEDE
THE STIGMATA—MARGARET EBNERIN—DISAPPEARANCE
OF THE MIRACULOUS WOUNDS DURING THE PROCESS OF
THEIR FORMATION—SAINT CATHARINE OF SIENA—UR-
SULA OF VALENTIA—HELEN OF HUNGARY—HIERONYME
CARVAGLIO—LIDUINA—THE COMPLETE STIGMATA—VE-
RONICA GIULIANI—JANE OF JESUS MARY—ELIZABETH OF
SPALBECK—GERTRUDE OF COSTEN—JANE OF THE CROSS
—HOW THE STIGMATA, HAVING BEEN FORMED, DISAP-
PEAR WHOLLY OR IN PART.

IT has sometimes been conjectured that the
earliest trace of the Stigmata exists in
the words of Saint Paul, "I bear the
marks of the Lord Jesus in my body;" but
the tradition of the Church cannot be appealed
to in support of this interpretation. It is far
more probable that the apostle alludes, in

this passage, to the illtreatment which he had
endured in the service of Christ. And further,
what renders the mystical interpretation of
this text still more doubtful is, that throughout the range of Christian antiquity we
do not meet with a single example of the
Stigmata, in the present acceptation of the
word.

The Stigmata is, in fact, a distinguishing
characteristic of the spiritual life in modern as
compared with ancient times. It is supposed
that Saint Francis of Assisi was the first who
bore in his own person the wounds of Christ.
This circumstance, therefore, induces us to
lay greater stress upon the event, and to
relate it at length, with all the details recorded
in certain authentic documents, which have
been handed down to us by S. Bonaventure
and other contemporary writers. By this
means we shall be enabled to form a more
complete idea of the phenomenon.

S. Francis of Assisi. Francis divided his life between
prayer and action. After hav-
ing been for a time absorbed in
most sublime contemplation, he
would turn to works of mercy in behalf of his
fellow-men. In order to pursue his medita-

tions with greater freedom, he was accustomed
to withdraw from time to time to Mount
Alverno, among the Apennines.   There,
upon one occasion, he fasted for forty days in
honour of the archangel Saint Michael, his
soul being rapt in prayer, and his heart burning with divine love.   Meanwhile he was
favoured with long and frequent ecstasies,
which illuminated him with light from on
high, and thus communing with God, he was
able to discern clearly the infinite majesty of
his Creator, and his own nothingness.

Two years before his death he imposed
upon himself the same fast on Mount Alverno, and as he was considering how he
should act in the future, in order to perfectly
fulfil the will of God, he received a secret
inspiration, urging him to open the Gospels,
for therein he should find the information he
so much desired.   In obedience to the bidding
of this interior voice, having first prayed, he
bade his companion open the book of the
Gospels upon the altar three times, in the
name of the Most Blessed Trinity.   Each
time the book opened at the part which
records the history of the Passion.   Then did
Francis understand what God required of him.

He saw that as he had hitherto striven to imitate the life of Jesus Christ, even so was he now called to be made like to Him in His sufferings and Passion. There was no hesitation on his part. Worn down as he was, and wasted by his penitential life, he instantly resolved to obey the voice of God without delay.

Accordingly, one morning, on the Feast of the Exaltation of the Holy Cross, while praying on the mountain steep, inflamed with a vehement desire of being crucified with his Lord and Saviour, he beheld a seraph descending towards him from heaven, borne upon six burning and radiant wings. When the celestial messenger had drawn near, he perceived the form of a crucified man between the wings, having his hands and feet extended. Two of the wings rose above his head, two were spread as for the purpose of flying, and the remaining two veiled his body.

Francis was greatly astonished at this sight; nevertheless he experienced much joy in beholding the vision with which God had been pleased to favour him, as well as deep sorrow, which emotion overcame him as he gazed . upon so terrible a spectacle, the sight of which seemed to pierce his heart as with a sword. One thing seemed to him incomprehensible. It was how to reconcile such an appearance of suffering with the notion of the impassibility of a seraph. The meaning, however, of the apparition was now made plain to him, and he discovered that his conformity with his Divine Master was to be brought about by means of the eager fire of love enkindled in his heart rather than by the actual martyrdom of his body.

When the vision had vanished from his sight, its effect was evidenced by the glow of divine energy which flooded his soul, as well as by the wonderful impressions which were stamped upon his flesh. For he bore in very truth upon his hands and feet the same appearance of the nails which he had beheld upon the form of the seraph, and in his right side there was a wound such as would be inflicted by a lance.

The wounds on his hands and feet widened considerably at one end, and they were bleeding. A nail, resembling one of iron, was set in the midst of each. These nails were formed in the flesh and cellular tissues; they were black and hard. The heads were placed uppermost, and the points were turned back, in such a manner, however, as to leave space enough for a finger to have been inserted between them and the skin. They were moveable every way, for if on one side they were pressed against the flesh, on the other they contrariwise projected. But they could not be withdrawn, as Saint Clare ascertained, for when she attempted to remove one after the death of the saint, all her efforts were ineffectual.

Francis could move his fingers notwithstanding the wounds, and he was able to use his hands and feet as before; but walking much became difficult, and for this reason he always rode on horseback in his later journeyings about the country. The wound in his side was deep, and about three inches in width, according to the statement of a brother who accidentally touched it. It was red, and the contraction of the flesh around it seems to have given it a circular form. The Saint's habit was often stained by the blood which flowed from it. The wounds never presented any appearance of canker or of suppuration, nor did Francis ever make use of any healing remedy. Nothing but a miracle could possibly have enabled him to live two years longer, considering his great sufferings and continual loss of blood.

When the holy man came down from the mountain, bearing the Stigmata of Jesus upon his members, he was much embarrassed as to the course he should pursue. He shrunk, on the one hand, from making public the hidden things of God; and yet he knew full well, on the other hand, that it would be impossible for him to hide his wounds from his companions. Before deciding whether to speak of them himself or not, he summoned a few of his most intimate friends, and exposed his doubts, but merely in general terms. Whereupon one of his hearers, gifted with more penetration than the rest, perceiving that something of an extraordinary nature had evidently befallen him, told him that this thing was not intended for his own spiritual advantage only, but for the edification of his neighbour also. Francis then determined no longer to withhold what might prove useful to others, and he related what had taken place on the Mount, adding, however, that certain words had been pronounced by Him who had

appeared to him, which he would never reveal to any one so long as he lived.

As to the wounds he bore, he hid them as
well as he could.   He always wore shoes
and stockings, and kept his hands carefully
covered.   But, notwithstanding every precaution, many of the Brethren saw what he
could not entirely conceal from them.   Pope
Alexander and several Cardinals testified as
ocular witnesses to the fact of his having
borne the Stigmata; and after his death it
was seen by more than fifty of the Brothers
of |his own Order, by Saint Clare and her
Sisters, as well as by a great concourse of lay-
persons who had flocked from all sides to
behold so great a marvel, and who were permitted to touch the miraculous wounds with
their own hands.   (See the Life of S. Francis, by S. Bonaventure, ch. xiii.-xv.)

**Margaret
Ebnerin.**
Thus we find that it pleased
God to bestow upon Saint Francis
at once what He yielded to others
only by degrees.   The marks upon the head,
and the wound in the heart, which usually
constitute two initiatory stages, are entirely
passed over, the feet and hands of the Saint
being stamped with the sacred imprints at

the very outset. The wounds were somewhat less painful in Saint Francis's case, owing perhaps to the way in which he had received them, but where their development was gradual they were more sensibly felt.

The life of Margaret Ebnerin affords most valuable information to persons desirous of knowing what may be the proximate dispositions of those upon whom the Stigmata is about to appear. She was born at Nuremberg, and led a holy life in the Convent of Mary Medingen, where she died in 1351. Only a portion of her life has as yet been published, the remainder is contained in manuscripts which may be found in ancient libraries.

Our Lord's Passion filled her with sentiments of such tender compassion, that the mere sight of a crucifix made her burst into tears, and she would weep till she was fairly exhausted. A simple meditation upon the Passion stirred the very depths of her soul, and this to such an extent, that she could not dwell upon the sufferings of Jesus without rousing in herself intolerable pains, both of body and soul, which wrung from her cries of anguish that might be heard all over the convent. At the same time clear fresh blood issued from her nose and mouth, and the state she fell into so alarmed those about her, that often, despairing of her recovery, they caused her to be anointed.

She writes as follows in her journal: " On Palm Sunday I heard our Sisters singing during the procession. Afterwards, when the Passion was being read at Mass, my heart and all my limbs were penetrated with such intense pain, and such piercing anguish, that I was completely overcome, and had to be supported. Then I broke forth into words, exclaiming plaintively amid my tears: Alas ! O Jesus, my good Master. Alas ! my sweet Love ! These words escaped me; I was unable to restrain my voice. But I cannot give any description of the love which consumed my heart, or of the ineffable sweetness which I experienced in the compassionate presence of God. Another time, on Good Friday, after Matins, I cried out three several times: Alas ! Jesus, my Lord. And I was overwhelmed with such deep sorrow, that nothing could afford me any consolation when I thought of all that our Saviour suffered for us upon this day. His Passion is as present to me as though I were actually watching the scenes with the eyes of the body, and the thought of it so completely fills my mind that I cannot dwell upon His eternal glory, or the beauty and splendour which now surround Him in heaven.

"Whilst the Sisters beside me tried to comfort me, I felt an interior suffering in my hands. It seemed as if they were being stretched, torn, and transpierced. I thought I should never be able to use them again. I also experienced an extraordinary sensation of pain in my head, as though something sharp had been driven into it. Moreover, it shook so violently, with a rapid trembling motion, that, in spite of all their efforts, it was as much as the Sister could do to support it all. I suffered from the same trembling again for a long while after Easter; it used to come over me whenever I prayed fervently, and when I read or spoke. And even now I still feel as though every portion of my frame, my side, my back, and all my bones especially, had been shattered. The agony of death seems to have taken hold of me,—and, in truth, what I undergo would suffice to kill me, if it were the Will of God."

One day our Lord made known to her the precise hour when the Bloody Sweat had fallen from Him in the Garden of Olives, as well as what He had suffered from that time until His death upon the cross. This revelation overwhelmed her anew with deep sorrow, which endured from Passion Sunday until the festival of Easter. Then, on Holy Saturday, just as the *Regina Cœli* was to be sung, it pleased God to restore her suddenly to health, to the great astonishment of every one. She found herself able to rise, to enter the choir, and so take part in the joys of the Resurrection. " For," said she, " our Lord knows full well that at this time consolations so sweet are vouchsafed to me, that I can neither write or speak of them, because none can understand them except God Himself and the soul upon whom He bestows them."

Saint Catharine of Siena. Margaret had suffered the pain of the wounds only. With her the Stigmata was neither visible nor lasting. It sometimes happens, however, that just as the imprints are upon the point of appearing, they vanish at the request of those who were to have been marked with them. This was the

case with Saint Catharine of Siena, according
to the statement of Raymond of Capua. It
seems that an event of a preparatory nature
occurred on the 18th of August, 1370.

After having received Holy Communion,
the Saint used to be wholly absorbed in God.
Her soul was steeped, so to speak, in the
ocean of His Divinity. It might have been
compared to a fish in water, immersed in,
and completely surrounded as it is, by that,
its native element. So entrancing to her was
the presence of her Creator, that she could
scarcely rouse herself in order to regain her
cell and her bed. After her return, however,
upon the occasion of which we speak, she
was raised up into the air in the presence of
three witnesses, and she then began to pro-
nounce, in a low voice, words so sweet, that
those who heard her could not but be much
affected by them. She next prayed for several
persons, for her confessor among others, and
although at the time he was far away, he was
conscious of the prayer she was making for
him.

As one of her hands was outstretched in
prayer, she appeared to suffer great pain in
it, exclaiming, according to her usual custom,

with a sigh,—"May Jesus Christ be praised."
Her confessor afterwards obliged her, in virtue of holy obedience, to relate what had
taken place, and she spoke thus. "When I
had earnestly prayed for your eternal salvation, God promised to grant my request.
Now I in no way distrusted His promise,
nevertheless, wishing to preserve some record
of it, I said: 'Lord, give me a token thereof.'
Whereupon He answered: 'Stretch forth
thy hand towards Me.' I did so; then He
took a nail and set the point of it in the
centre of my hand. He pressed so firmly
upon the nail that it seemed to pierce my
hand. I felt as much pain as though it had
been driven in with a hammer. Thus, therefore, thanks be to God, I now bear the Wound
of the Right Hand. It cannot be seen, but
I feel it intensely, and it ever pains me."

Later on she went to Pisa, accompanied by
Raymond and some others. She was hos-
pitably entertained by an inhabitant of the
town, who dwelt near to the church of St.
Christina. "On Sunday," continues Raymond, "I celebrated Mass there and gave
her Holy Communion. After this she remained for a long time in ecstasy, as usual.

We waited until she should come to herself, hoping to receive some spiritual consolations from her. As we were watching her, we saw her suddenly arise from her recumbent posture, and then, kneeling down, she stretched out her arms and hands. Her face was bright and beaming. For a long space she remained thus motionless, with her eyes closed. Then, as though she had received a mortal wound, she fell down abruptly. After the lapse of a few moments she appeared to resume the use of her limbs, and having sent for me, she said in a low voice: 'Father, I would you should know that, thanks to the mercy of our Lord Jesus Christ, I bear His Stigmata upon my body.' I answered that I had conjectured such to be the case from all that I had observed to take place during her ecstasy. I then inquired what our Lord had been pleased to do. 'I saw my crucified Saviour,' she replied, 'descending towards me in the midst of a flood of light, and the effort which my soul made to advance and meet my Creator forced my body to arise. Then I beheld bleeding jets coming directly upon me from the five openings of the Sacred Wounds of our Lord; they were darting

towards my hands, my feet, and my heart.
I comprehended the full meaning of the mystery, and I exclaimed: 'I beseech Thee let
not the scars appear outwardly upon my
body.' While I was yet speaking, the blood-
stained rays grew bright and shining, and
when they actually struck the five portions of
my body, namely, my hands, my feet, and my
heart, it was in the form of light.' 'But
did not any ray of light,' I asked, 'strike
you upon the right side?' She answered,
'No, the ray fell upon my left side immediately over my heart. The line of light
which proceeded from the right side of our
Lord did not strike me obliquely, but main-
tained a straight course.' I then inquired
whether she did not feel great pain in all
these places. She answered me with a deep
sigh, saying, 'I feel such violent pain in
these five spots, but more especially in my
heart, that unless another miracle came to
my assistance, it would seem to me impossible to exist in such a state.'"

Shortly after this she fell into a deep fainting fit, more alarming than any she had yet
had, so that her friends, whose compassion
moved them to tears, began to fear for her

life. When she recovered consciousness she said that she now clearly perceived that without special aid from the hand of God she must very soon die.

All these events occurred in the presence of the General of the Dominican Order, Thomas della Ponte, who had been her first confessor, and who was related to her. There were present also Bartholomew Montucci, a gentleman of Siena, and a very learned man; Antony, Count of Elcio, who was afterwards a bishop in Sicily; Doctor Raynier Paglianesi, of Siena; Augustine of Siena, a very celebrated preacher; Dr. Simon de Cascina, and Bartholomew of St. Dominic, who was at a later period made Bishop of Carona in Greece. Witnesses such as these afford us reliable evidence, for they were all men eminently well qualified to form an opinion concerning what they had seen.

The same thing befel several others likewise. Sister Ursula of Valentia, known also as Ursula Aguir, at an **Ursula Aguir.** early date received the crown of thorns, accompanied by great suffering. It was bestowed, however, invisibly. She afterwards received the wound in the heart in the same way. The fact was evidenced by cramp and violent palpitations, and by fits of suffocation and by swoons. Any moment might have been her last, and the pain she suffered was inexpressible. At length, one day, as she was praying in a church, on the Feast of S. Benedict, in 1592, S. Catharine appeared to her, holding a crucifix. The nails detached themselves, and came and fixed themselves upon the hands and feet of Ursula. She fainted away, but as soon as she recovered her senses she earnestly entreated our Lord to allow the pain only to remain with her, and to remove the outward impression of the Stigmata which had just been set upon her. Her prayer was heard. Her sufferings and fainting fits returned every Friday, but no trace of any mark whatever was perceptible upon her hands and feet. (Marchese, Sept. 8, p. 79.)

Helen of Hungary. Upon a certain day Helen of Hungary, as she was rapt in contemplation of the Passion, saw a circlet of gold resting over our Lord's head, from the midst of which rose a lily as white as snow. While she was looking up she perceived a ray of light, dyed with blood, descending from the cross upon her right hand. Seeing it, she cried out, saying, "Lord, let not the wound be visible." Her petition was granted at that time, but afterwards the Stigmata were imprinted upon her. (Steill. Nov. 9, p. 87.)

Hieronyme Carvaglio. Hieronyme Carvaglio had long desired to participate in the sufferings of Jesus, and at length her wish was gratified. It came to pass one day, as she was begging for this grace interiorly with great fervour, that she beheld five jets of blood, mingled with fire, descending from heaven. They were directed towards her, and the desire of her heart was fulfilled by means of them, for she could feel all the pain of the wounds in her hands and feet without bearing any exterior mark of them, whereas a large open wound appeared upon her left side, which shed quantities of blood, particularly on Fridays. Now this was precisely what she had prayed for, because the wound in her side could easily be concealed by her garments. (Marchese, October, p. 234.)

Liduina. Our Lord Jesus Christ Himself imprinted His Stigmata upon the body of Liduina. He first appeared to her in the shape of a child in a vision. He gazed upon her tenderly, and then suddenly assumed the form of our suffering Redeemer. Amazed at the sight, and overcome with feelings both of joy and sorrow, her spirit was borne away into the radiant light which beamed forth from Him, and whilst she was thus entranced with rapturous delight in His divine presence she received the impression of the Five Wounds. But dreading lest such outward tokens should attract the gaze of the curious multitude, and possibly become to herself an occasion of vain-glory, she begged for their removal, saying, " Grant, O Lord, I beseech Thee, that this, the token of Thy love, may be known but to Thyself and to me." A new skin instantly formed over the wounds, and no vestige of them remained beyond the pain they caused and a light shade of pallor.

So it was with Magdalen of Pazzi. Burning rays had communicated to her the pain of the Five Wounds, which she joyfully endured, but no external mark was manifest. (See her Life, ch. ii. p. 4.) Saint Coleta, Mechtilde of Stanz, and Columba Rocasini, are other examples. (Steill. Jan. 27, March 10.)

In the case of Margaret Columna, the wound in the side was apparent, but all the rest were invisible; whereas Blanche de Gazineau, who died in 1564, was marked with the Stigmata visibly upon one foot only. (Steill. Jan. 11.)

God does not, sometimes, answer the prayers of His Saints in
this matter, at least not instan-
Veronica Giuliani.
taneously, but He allows the impression of His Wounds to appear upon their body. Veronica Giuliani's experience affords an instance of this, and it is from her own narrative that we derive our knowledge of all that took place when she received the sacred Stigmata. The wound in her side was reopened at Christmas in the year 1696. (It appears that she had already received it, and that it had closed again.) At the same date she was further told by God Himself that she would receive the other Wounds on Good Friday in the following year, when it should fall on the 5th of April. Accordingly, on that day we find her writing as follows in her journal: "April 5th. This night, whilst I was making my meditation, our risen Lord appeared to me with His Blessed Mother and the Saints, as

they have oftentimes been manifest to me before. He commanded me to confess my sins, which I did, beginning with these words: 'I have sinned against Thee, O my God, and I now confess it in Thy presence.' But scarcely had I thus spoken when the extreme violence of the grief which overwhelmed me, as I thought of all the outrages of which I had been guilty against God, forced me to stop. Our Lord then desired my angel guardian to proceed for me. He obeyed, and placing his hand upon my head, he spoke in my name, saying: ' O eternal God, sovereign Judge of all, I stand before Thee in obedience to Thy command, that I may speak in the name of this Virgin, for the sake of her eternal salvation. I confess to Thee all those sins which she has committed in thought, in word, and in deed.' While he was thus speaking, I seemed to see myself surrounded by all the sins which I had ever committed during the whole course of my life. Nevertheless our Lord did not turn away His face from me; on the contrary, His countenance was serene and merciful, and I felt assured that He was inclined to pardon me. Then He showed me the Wounds in His Hands and His Side. As

my good Angel confessed my gravest sins the
grief in my soul augmented, but our Lord
encouraged me Himself, saying, 'I forgive
thee, and I blot out in My Blood all the sins
which thou hast committed during thy life.' I
was then rapt higher still, for He drew my
spirit up to Himself. I could see all my sins
distinctly, and the vision of them filled my
soul with sorrow and regret. I began, however, to perceive that as my Angel enumerated
my sins they disappeared, a circumstance
which infused great confidence into me, for I
comprehended that my heart was undergoing
its purification conformably to the will of God,
and in virtue of the merits of the most holy
Wounds of Jesus.

"O my God! how could I speak or write of
what passed within me, upheld as I thus was
in that excess of Thy love! I can but speak
of the effects that love wrought in me, and of
the infinite sorrow I felt for my sins. Could I
have cancelled them by enduring all the tor-
ments of the martyrs, or by taking upon myself all the sufferings which men have borne
from the beginning of the world to this day,
together with those they will have yet to bear
until the end of time, willingly would I have

4

done so. My Angel concluded my confession by a general accusation, and finally presented me to our Lord purified, who arose, saying, 'Go in peace, and sin no more.' Then He gave me His blessing, and the vision instantly disappeared."

When consciousness returned the Saint continued to give utterance to the same sentiments which she had entertained during her ecstasy. She incessantly repeated, "More, more sufferings, more crosses." Taking a crucifix, she pressed it to her heart, amorously kissing the sacred Wounds, and beseeching our Lord to permit her to share in the pain He had suffered in each one of them. Her heart became more and more vehemently inflamed, and beat violently, as though it were about to spring forth from its confinement in her breast, and thus she soon relapsed into the same state of ecstasy as before, and seemed to be sinking into her last agony. She recovered, however, an hour later, and began to pray, and during this her prayer she received the Stigmata.

Again she was ravished into an ecstasy for the third time, and our Lord appeared to her, fastened to the cross, with His Mother at His

feet. Veronica besought the most holy Virgin
to intercede for her, for of herself she could
do nothing. Our Blessed Lady promised to
do so, and upon this a very clear light was
instantly bestowed upon the Saint, which
made her own nothingness distinctly visible
to her. Meanwhile, our Lord assured her that
He would render her in all things like to
Himself. Three times He asked her what she
desired, and three times she replied that her
only desire was to be crucified with Him.
"It shall be granted thee," He answered;
"but from this time forth thou must be ever
faithful to Me. And for this I give thee the
grace needful, by means of these wounds,
which I now engrave upon thy body as a
token of the gift which I bestow upon thee."
Five brilliant rays of light immediately issued
from the Five Wounds of our Lord towards
her. She could distinguish little flames descending in them. Four of these flames contained the nails, and the fifth the lance. Both
the nails and the lance appeared to be of gold,
but they were nevertheless flaming. The
heart of the Saint was transpierced, as were
also her hands and feet. In the midst of
intense pain she felt herself being wholly

transformed into her Divine Lord. The
flames returned to the rays whence they had
come forth.

When she was restored to consciousness
she found her arms extended and stiff. She
tried to look at the wound in her side, but
could not succeed in doing so on account of
the pain in her hands. After several attempts,
however, she at length effected her purpose,
and found the wound not only open, but
shedding blood and water. In obedience to
the command of her confessor she was afterwards obliged to undergo a very strict examination, the conduct of which was entrusted
to Eustace, Bishop of the diocese, by the tri-
bunal of the Roman Inquisition. This was
undertaken in order to certify the truth, or to
expose what would otherwise have been a
most detestable fraud.

The measures adopted by the Bishop were
such that no imposture could possibly have
escaped detection. In the first place, he endeavoured to ascertain whether Veronica was
patient, humble, and submissive, for these
virtues are the distinguishing mark of the
operation of the Spirit of God. He deprived
her of her charge as mistress of the Novices ;

he interdicted her, and reprimanded her so loudly in the parlour that his voice was audible in the cloisters of the Convent. He treated her as though she had been a witch or excommunicated, and even went so far as to threaten to have her burnt in the midst of the enclosure. The only companion permitted her was a lay Sister, named Frances, who was ordered to treat her harshly as a supposed hypocrite and sorceress, nor was she to allow her to speak to the other Sisters. During a certain interval she was refused Holy Communion, and the Abbess fixed the amount of time she was to spend in the confessional. Whilst the case was pending the Bishop called in several physicians to heal her wounds. Having previously bandaged her hands, they enveloped them in gloves, which they sealed up. These experiments were carried on until late in the month of October, but the wounds, far from healing, only became larger still. Meanwhile the Saint was true to herself throughout the entire ordeal. No sign of weakness once escaped her. She was invariably humble and resigned, calm and self-forgetful, and she made no complaint concerning the ill-treatment to which she was sub-

jected. The Inquisition finally, after receiving the Bishop's reports, declared itself satisfied, and Veronica was left in peace. (Her
Life, by Salvatori, pp. 99, 108, and 174.)

Jane of Jesus-Mary. Jane of Jesus-Mary submitted to no less severe an in-
vestigation. As if by way of
prelude to the bestowal of the sacred Stigmata, she, in common with most of those who
have received it, was first offered two crowns,
one of thorns and one of flowers. She chose
the former, and from that day forward until
the hour of her death she suffered from such
excruciating headaches that her skull could
literally be heard cracking, as though it had
been interiorly shattered. She very soon
participated in all the sufferings of the Passion
of Jesus. Week by week, from six o'clock on
Thursday evening until the same hour on
Friday, she was wholly absorbed in meditating upon the scenes of that unutterable woe.
As the successive hours and moments passed
she seemed to be following out each several
act of our Lord's long agony, and to be
enduring the same pain which He, the object
of her contemplation, had Himself endured.
At first her sufferings were confined to her

soul, being excited by means of the tender
compassion which the Passion of her Beloved,
aroused within her. But after a while the
subtle cord which binds the soul and body
together communicated the sufferings of the
former to the latter. Her pains now gathered
with intenser force round certain central
points, and began to manifest themselves by
exterior signs.

She was still living in the married state,
when, at the age of nineteen, on the 17th of
February, 1613, being the Sunday preceding
Lent, she received Holy Communion. After
this she became absorbed anew in profound
meditation upon the sufferings of Jesus, and
an ardent desire of sharing in them was
kindled within her. Her longing was gratified. She fell into ecstasy, and in addition to
the pains she had already borne in her head,
she obtained those which affect the hands, the
feet, and the side. No change occurred again
for about two years and three months. Then,
upon the 8th of May, the Feast of the Apparition of the Archangel Saint Michael, her
hands closed, and that so firmly that the
physicians who attempted it tried in vain to
open them. They were obliged at length to

admit the supernatural view of the case, and therefore declared it to be one which did not depend upon human aid for its cure.

She remained in the same condition for eleven days, until the evening of Ascension Day, the 19th of May, when she was again rapt in ecstasy, after having earnestly desired to participate in the sufferings of the Passion. Upon this our Lord appeared to her crucified, and wonderfully bright red rays fell from His wounds towards her. Her soul was plunged into the delicious fire of divine charity, but her body was a prey to such acute anguish that she was bathed in sweat from head to foot, and cast down upon the ground in mortal agony. She was not aware that night of what had taken place, but the next morning, when she would have approached the holy table, she fell into a fainting fit, and a cold sweat broke out over her. She had to be borne away, and when those who tended her endeavoured to unclose her hands, they found them to be marked with the imprints of the Stigmata.

Shortly after she received the crown of thorns as well. An apparition was manifest to her while she was engaged in prayer, and when she afterwards removed her veil she discovered that her head was encircled by two lines, one of which was deeper than the other. In the centre of this circle was a swelling which occasioned her much pain. Her humility prompted her to consider this circumstance as the result of some accident, and she accordingly consulted two of the most distinguished physicians of the town, Aspe and Oliva. They however agreed in declaring that they knew of nothing in the ordinary course which could produce such an effect.

When the fact was reported abroad, it was not at once credited without further examination into the truth of the story. Ferdinand d'Azevedo, Archbishop of Burgos, and President of Castile, having heard it, ordered his grand vicar, Manriquez, to make a careful inquiry, and to draw up a report, which was to be sent to him, concerning the matter. In pursuance of this command, Manriquez, on the 16th of February, 1618, assembled a body of witnesses. It was composed of the commissary of the Inquisition, the suffragan Bishop, several Abbots and Priors in the district, certain parish priests and scientific men, a soldier, some tradespeople belonging to the town, and two physicians, Aspe and Pacheco.

Jane appeared and manifested her wounds in their presence, so that each one in turn was enabled to examine them attentively. She first showed them her hands, which they all carefully surveyed. Both were marked with a wound, which was neither round nor square, but nearly triangular in form. Although not very deep, it was sufficiently so for the flesh to be laid bare, for the outer skin was rent. A whitish humour stood like dew over the centre. These wounds had not penetrated to the other side of her hands, and no swelling or alteration of any kind was perceptible around them. The condition of the surrounding flesh was perfectly healthy. They proceeded to wash one of her wounds, employing a sponge and some water, and then, at Pacheco's suggestion, soap was used, and that so forcibly as to occasion her violent pain, but she betrayed no outward sign of what she was undergoing.

Aspe deposed that he had seen these wounds before, nearly two years and a half ago, and that moreover he, together with Oliva, had undertaken their treatment at that time.

Despite every remedy, however, that could be applied, they had remained unaltered, in fact, precisely what they were at the present moment.

Jane was now told to show her feet, and she placed them for that purpose upon a small stool. There was a wound upon the instep, which appeared to be deeper than the wounds in her hands, but which was bedewed with the same moisture. Upon the other side, that is, in the soles of her feet, there was a still deeper wound, presenting, however, the same total absence of any appearance of disease or tumour of any kind.

They then constrained her to uncover her breast as far as might be, and a much larger wound, on the left side underneath the chest, was disclosed to view. It was not only larger than the others, but was differently shaped likewise; it was deeper also, and yielded a greater quantity of blood. The inspection of her head next occupied their attention. Having drawn back her veil, they found her forehead encircled with a ring about an inch wide, which projected from the skin. When this was touched and pressed with the finger it yielded beneath the pressure, as though it

were swollen, and so formed an indentation
half an inch deep all round, which, in the
opinion of the physicians, must have reached
the skull.

The medical men, having completed their
examination, pronounced that the wounds
were not produced by natural causes, neither
could they be the effect of any attempted
imposture. At a later period they endorsed
this statement upon oath, in writing, adding
at the same time the reasons which had in-
duced them to come to their conclusion. All
the other persons present were much struck
by what they had beheld. They admired the
great virtues which adorned Jane no less than
the miracles she had wrought, which had been
witnessed by several among them. They
unanimously agreed in regard to the verdict
of the physicians, and proceeded to confirm
their testimony. An official report, signed
by all the commissioners, was immediately
drawn up, which was deposited in the Fran-
ciscan church at Burgos, as soon as the result
of the inquiry had been communicated to the
Archbishop.

This did not, however, fully satisfy him,
and in the year following he went himself

to Burgos, where, having made all necessary inquiries, he sent for Jane. He then examined her wounds, one by one, with scrupulous care, in the presence of trustworthy witnesses. He was informed by her that the marks of the Stigmata had at first appeared upon the upper part of her hands, but that she had prayed to God to remove them on account of their exposure to the public gaze. This her prayer had been heard. After his searching examination was ended, the Archbishop's own opinion coincided with that of the Commissioners, and he drew up a formal declaration to that effect. (See Acts of her Life, printed at Cologne in 1682, pp. 158-187.)

The same thing has occurred in many other instances. We may cite, as an example, a Cistercian Nun, Elizabeth of Spalbeck,

Elizabeth of Spalbeck.

who was ravished out of herself seven times a day, in accordance with the number of the canonical hours. When she was in this state, neither breath nor motion, nor any action of the senses whatsoever could be perceived in her. She bled, moreover, almost every day, but especially on Fridays. (Annals of Citeaux, Oct. 19.)

Gertrude D'Oosten. Another case is that of Gertrude D'Oosten, of Delf. A year beforehand a certain Béguine, Lielta, had predicted what would befall her, but Gertrude would not believe it. But notwithstanding her incredulity, while she was praying before her crucifix on Holy Thursday night, in the year 1340, the Sacred Wounds were, as she felt, set upon her. Blood flowed from them seven times a day, corresponding with the canonical hours. So extraordinary an occurrence could not long be concealed; and such a multitude of people thronged about her, that she could scarcely find time to attend to her spiritual exercises. Dreading, moreover, lest she should yield to some passing impulse of vain glory, she besought God to remove the imprints which He had stamped upon her. He was pleased to accede to her request, and thenceforth her blood ceased to flow, and the scars were the only remaining trace of the miraculous wounds. But she suffered intense pain in the region of the heart, and she lost, as indeed she had done during the whole of the time her wounds were bleeding, all feeling of the sweetness with which she had been for-

merly inundated. She once more conceived
an ardent desire of being healed, but her
prayers in this respect remained unanswered.
(Sponde. A.D. 1340.)

Jane of the Cross received the
Stigmata on the morning of **Jane of**
Good Friday, in the year 1524. **the Cross.**
Nothing further happened until Ascension
Day, but the wounds only appeared on
Fridays and on Saturdays. With the approach of Sunday her pain ceased, and the
imprints themselves vanished entirely away,
leaving no trace of their existence. They
were round, about the size of a real. Their
hue was rose-colour, and they diffused a
sweet smell; whereas the wounds of Apol-
lonaria de Volaterra, which had yielded a bad
odour during life, only became fragrant after
her death. In one instance, that of Sister
Pieron, of the Third Order of St. Francis,
the marks of the Stigmata assumed a grey or
blackish shade. They were prominent, and
were set in the centre of her hands, but they
did not penetrate to the other side, neither
did blood flow from them, although they were
exceedingly painful. Thus it would appear

that the formation in her case was much what it was in that of Saint Francis himself.

Stephanie Quinzani, who was born at Soncino in 1457, shared in the Passion of our Lord every Friday. His Sacred Wounds were imprinted upon her body, and the crown of thorns was manifest upon her head. Oftentimes she would seem to feel a wheel turning within her heart.

Queen Margaret of Hungary was likewise stamped with the Wounds of Christ. This fact having been called in question some time after her death, Pope Innocent the Fourth ordered her body to be exhumed, and the wounds were then exposed to view, as red and as fresh as though she were still living. (Steill. t. i., p. 30.)

Osanna of Mantua furnishes us with another instance. She too was marked with the sacred Stigmata, which may still be seen upon her body, for it continues in perfect preservation to this day.

In most cases we find the wounds to have been produced by means of burning, blood-stained rays of light. They were thus bestowed upon Columba Rocasani and Anne of Vargas, in the Convent of St. Catharine, at

Vallisolet, in Spain; as also upon Mary of Lisbon, upon Jane of Verceil, Magdalen of Pazzi, and Stephanie Quinzani; which last sweated blood on Fridays, and often bore the Five Wounds in addition to the Crown of Thorns, and the Stripes of the Flagellation. (Steill. t. ii., p. 122; t. i. p. 10.)

Peter of Alva, author of a work on the subject, entitled "*Prodigium Naturæ, portentum gratiæ,*" reckons up thirty-five persons marked with the complete Stigmata; but the instances which might be advanced would amount to twice that number.

We will mention, as being less generally known, the names of Christina, a contemporary of Denis the Carthusian; Mary Razzi, or Raggia, born at Chios in 1532; Philippa of St. Thomas, at Montemor in Portugal, and Elizabeth of Reith, at Waldsee, in Allgau. The three latter were Dominicans. Also Stieva, at Ham, in Westphalia; Sister Mary of the Incarnation, a Carmelite at Pontoise; Margaret Bruch, in the village of Endringen, near Constance, who lived about 1503; Bridget of Holland, of the Third Order of Saint Dominic, about 1590; and Mary of

Saint Dominic, and Lucy of Narni, Dominicans likewise. (Steill. Jan. 4, May 14, and
Nov. 15.)

CHAPTER III.

𝔥𝔬𝔴 𝔱𝔥𝔢 𝔖𝔱𝔦𝔤𝔪𝔞𝔱𝔞, 𝔬𝔫𝔠𝔢 𝔣𝔬𝔯𝔪𝔢𝔡, 𝔡𝔦𝔰𝔞𝔭𝔭𝔢𝔞𝔯𝔰 𝔴𝔥𝔬𝔩𝔩𝔶 𝔬𝔯 𝔦𝔫 𝔭𝔞𝔯𝔱.

SAINT IDA—THE FLAGELLATION—ARCHANGELA OF TAR-
DERA—LUTGARD—PERIODS OF LIFE AT WHICH THE STIG-
MATA IS PRODUCED—ANGELA OF PEACE—LUCY OF NARNI
—HELEN OF HUNGARY—MEN WHO HAVE RECEIVED THE
STIGMATA—BENEDICT OF RHEGIO—CHARLES OF SAETA—
ANGELO DE PAS—MATTHEW CARERI—AGOLINO OF
MILAN—THE LAY BROTHER DODONIUS—PHILIP OF
AQUERIA, ETC.

IT often happens that the imprints of the
Stigmata disappear at the request of
those who have received them, after a
perfect formation, and after having remained
apparent for a length of time. This was the
case, as we have already seen, with Gertrude
d'Oosten, Dominica of Paradise, Jane of the
Cross, and many others.

Ida of Louvain. Ida of Louvain, who died in the
year 1300, had certain circles of
various hues, which projected from

within and from without, in those parts of
her hands and feet which corresponded to the
spots in which our Blessed Lord was pierced
with the nails. So Hugh, her biographer,
relates, whose knowledge was derived from
manuscripts left by her confessor. In her
side, moreover, there was a wide, oblong-
shaped wound, through which her breath often
penetrated to the region of the liver. Nor
was this all; so intense and piercing was the
pain she suffered, that she could not bear the
contact of her very garments, nor of anything
else whatever, and for this reason she was
obliged to give up spinning, although it furnished her with the means of subsistence; for
the pain she endured prevented her from
supporting her distaff against her side. Her
hands and feet, too, were so exceedingly painful in those parts where the circles projected,
that no one could lay a finger on them, however lightly, or touch them in any way, without causing her very great suffering. Her
head was encircled with another wound, and
the crown of thorns seemed to be traceable in
its outline.

Her piety, however, so very much dis-
pleased her father, that he left her no peace,

and every time that he, or some other one of her relatives, did her some fresh injury, the pain of her wounds became intolerable. After a time she found that neither surgeons nor doctors could afford her any relief, and she tried to conceal the wonderful imprints as much as possible, especially those upon her hands, which were naturally most exposed to view. But she soon discovered that all her efforts were useless, for the pain forced her to betray somewhat of the anguish she endured, and the necessity, moreover, of earning her own livelihood prevented her from keeping her hands continually covered up.

Fearing, as indeed it proved, that the rumour of such a miraculous occurrence would spread, and would cause her to be much spoken of, she implored Almighty God to relieve her of this dread, and to remove the marks of the Stigmata. Her prayer was partly answered, for the excrescences disappeared, but a portion of the pain they caused remained, and throughout the rest of her life, whenever she met with things of a painful nature, or was attacked by hatred of any kind, the pain augmented, and thus afforded her an opportunity of practising patience. (A. S., April 13.)

Sometimes persons marked with the sacred imprints have obtained the removal of the more apparent ones by means of importunate prayer. Thus the wounds upon the hands will vanish, whilst those impressed upon the feet, being much more easily concealed, have been left. This would explain the case of a Cistercian Nun, named Catharine, who bore the divine impress upon her feet only; and we may also cite, as another instance, Blanch Gusman, daughter of Count Arias de Pagavedra. With her the Stigmata was imprinted upon one foot.

Sometimes, but this is very rare, the four wounds appertaining to the hands and feet are grouped round the wound in the heart, as in the case of a Tertiary, named Masrona, who led a very holy life near Grenoble, in 1627. The pious women who laid out her body after death discovered a wound near the heart, which was pronounced by the medical men who examined her to be a supernatural one. It would seem to have been composed of all the five Wounds combined. The one in the centre was round and crimson tinted, and the others were set about it in the form of a square. (De Stigmatismo sacro et profano. T. Raynaudi, S.J., p. 232.)

In the cases of which we have now spoken the phenomenon loses somewhat of its marked and distinct character. But this note returns, and even deepens, when the traces of our Saviour's Flagellation are imprinted upon the body, as in the case of Archangela Tardera, in Sicily, about the year 1608.

Archangela Tardera. When absorbed in prayer and meditation, she was frequently favoured with ecstasies and visions. For thirty-six years she was a prey to sufferings and maladies of every kind, such as cramp, fainting fits, and palpitation of the heart. She bore all, however, with patience and resignation. To add to her afflictions, she lost her sight during the last four years of her life, but she continued none the less cheerful and content. Besides the gift of prophecy and the discerning of spirits, she obtained the imprints of the Stigmata. They appeared upon her, covered over with skin of roseate hue. Notwithstanding all she had undergone, her thirst after suffering remained unabated, and she now begged to receive the

stripes of the Flagellation. This her prayer
was granted. She lay for a long time outstretched, scarcely breathing. Her body was
dislocated from head to foot, and was completely covered with bruises, contusions,
swellings, and stripes, such as would be produced by rods and lashes, so that every
moment seemed likely to be her last. But
nothing could quench her love of suffering:
it continued with her to the end of her life.
Her tomb was opened several times after her
death, and her body was always found in-
corrupt, with the divine seals of the Stigmata
imprinted upon its members. (Menolog. of
S. Francis, Sept., p. 1810.)

Whenever Saint Lutgard was
occupied in contemplating the Pas- **Lutgard.**
sion during her ecstasy, it seemed to her that
her own body was bathed in blood. A priest
who had discovered such to be the case,
watched his opportunity, and succeeded in
finding her in this state. She was leaning
against a wall, so that he was able to approach
her, and to examine her face and hands,
which were the only portions of her body
visible. They appeared to him to be covered
with blood recently shed, and drops of blood

were flowing from her hair likewise. He severed one lock, and taking it to the light, gazed at it in deep amazement. But when Lutgard recovered consciousness, the hair which the priest still held in his hand regained its natural colour.

The same thing is related of Catharine de Ricci, of Florence, who died in 1590, according to the testimony of Albert Casejus, the General of her Order, who saw her when he visited the convent in which she dwelt. Helen Brumsin, who died in the Convent of Desenhofen, in 1285, asked our Lord to bestow on her the sufferings of the Flagellation; whereupon she experienced such intense pain in every limb that she could not but believe her request had been granted. (Steill. Oct. 29, and May 31.)

Angela of Peace. The bestowal of the divine Wounds is not confined to any special period of life. Angela of Peace was but nine years old when, entering a church with one of her companions upon a certain day, she left her side to go and pray alone in a chapel dedicated to Saint Francis. While kneeling there, as she beheld the representation of the Saint bear-

ing the impression of the sacred Stigmata,
she began, with child-like simplicity, to
speak to him as though he were alive.
"Father," said she, "who gave you those
wounds? I cannot bear to see them, and
if you will let me, I will cure them for
you." "They are no wounds," replied St.
Francis, "they are gems." "But how can
they be gems?" said the child; "they are
bleeding." "They are jewels nevertheless,
in very truth," again spoke the voice in
answer, "and if you like, I will show you
how I received them." "I should like it
much," said Angela.

Instantly the vaulted roof of the chapel
appeared to open, and the Saint signed to her
to raise her eyes. She did so, and saw our
Lord in the form of a child, with His arms
outstretched upon a cross; she herself, meanwhile, was encompassed with a flood of light.
The vision approached her, and imprinted the
marks of the Stigmata upon her body, which
occasioned her such sensible pain that, uttering a piercing cry, she fell down, as though
dead, to the ground. She lay thus until the
evening, still surrounded by a bright light.
At length her friend returned, and finding

her in the midst of such a blaze of light, she took her to be on fire. Her cries summoned certain persons to the spot, and they bore away the child, still lost in ecstasy, to her parents. The doctors who were called in felt her pulse, but they could not move her arm.

Her mother, in attempting to support her, uncovered her hand, and they then discovered that it, as well as the other, was wounded. They inspected her feet also, and found that they too were wounded and bleeding. Various remedies were administered to rouse her, for her state was supposed to result from the wounds she had received, but all in vain. She continued in the same condition for eight days, and then she was restored to consciousness. When she found her mother was looking at her, weeping, she said to her: "Do not cry, for this is God's appointment; but send away the doctors, for they can do nothing for me." She lay for two years after this upon her bed, and was a prey to terrible sufferings. In the end she was abandoned by her own relations. She was, however, eventually healed, and her cure was no less miraculous than the bestowal of her wounds had been. (Marchese, t. v., p. 514.)

Lucy of Narni received the Stigmata when she was twenty years of age. Veronica Giuliani was thirty-seven, and Jane of the Cross forty-three. Another Jane of the Cross of Roveredo received the divine impressions only a few days before her death, and they continued red and bleeding even after she was dead. In the case of Helen of Hungary, on the contrary, they disappeared shortly before she died; they were taken from her in a vision.

Although we find that our Divine Lord's Wounds are more rarely imprinted upon men than upon women, nevertheless men are not excluded from the privilege of bearing them. It would suffice to instance St. Francis of Assisi alone, but many others have been thus highly favoured likewise. Benedict of Rhegio, a **Benedict of Rhegio.** Capuchin, was engaged in meditating upon the Passion, at Bologna, in the year 1602, when a thorn from the Redeemer's crown entered into his head, and penetrated even to the skull. The ardent love which consumed him became more intense as the wound widened, and wet cloths had to be applied in order to afford him some relief. (Menolog. of St. Francis, p. 2080.)

Charles of Saeta. Charles of Saeta, or Sazia, had the Wound in the side. Though but a lay brother, and quite illiterate, he was the author, by divine inspiration, of several mystical books. He was one day devoutly assisting at Mass, in the year 1648, when, at the Elevation, he beheld, with spiritual vision, a fiery dart, which sprang from the Sacred Host, and wounded his heart as with a hot iron. From that time forward he was tortured with excruciating anguish, intermingled, however, with such divine sweetness that his whole soul became inebriated with the love of God. The wound continued to be visible for many years, and only closed at length in answer to his persevering prayer to that effect. (Ibid., p. 383.)

Angelo de Pas. Angelo de Pas, of Perpignan, a Friar Minor, who experienced the sufferings of the Passion during life, bore the Wound of the heart as well. This was not discovered until after his decease, as the acts of the process, which was commenced for his canonization, record.

A corresponding case was that of Matthew Careri, of Mantua, but in this instance the wound was **Matthew Careri.** not a visible one. When the body of Agolino of Milan was examined, fifty years after his death, it was found in- **Agolino.** corrupt, as were also his garments, and on one side of his chest there was an open wound, which was bleeding. A similar wound was discovered upon the body of Cherubino of Aviliana, of the Augustinian Order. He had concealed it during life, as did likewise Melchior d'Arazil, at Valentia.

It came to pass one day, as the Venerable James Stephen was praying before the tabernacle, that there came forth from it a ray of light in the shape of an arrow, which struck his heart. Whereupon he was cast to the ground half dead, in a mingled transport of joy and pain, and while in this state the sacred wound of our Lord's side was found imprinted upon his breast. (Sylos. History of the Regular Canons, p. ii. 1. 13.)

Gautier of Strasburg, of the Order of Friars Preachers, who died in 1264, felt all the pains of the Five Wounds, but they were not visibly marked upon him. One day, when he was meditating upon our Lord's Passion, he for the first time experienced these mysterious pains; and upon another occasion, as he was contemplating the sorrows of the Blessed Virgin at the foot of the cross, he felt as though his heart were pierced with swords. (Steill. March 27.)

Saint Francis of Assisi, in a vision, in the year 1430, imprinted his own divine Stigmates upon the body of Robert de Malatesta, a descendant of the Rimini dynasty, who had abdicated his rulership in order to assume the habit of the Third Order of St. Francis. (Menolog. of St. Francis, Oct., p. 1950.)

Dodonius, a lay brother in the Premonstratensian Order, was marked with the Five Wounds; and they appeared also upon the body of Brother Nicholas of Ravenna after his death. John Graio the Martyr, of the Third Order of St. Francis, bore the wounds of the feet; they were two inches and a half wide, and proportionately long. Philip of

Philip of Aqueria. Aqueria, when meditating upon the Passion before his crucifix, experienced an ardent desire of participating in our Saviour's sufferings. Jets of blood, like so many arrows, instantly sprang from the wounds on the crucifix, and his hands, his feet, and his side were covered with blood in a most marvellous manner. From that day forward he endured all the agonies of the Passion. The image of the Crucified was so deeply graven within him as to be ever present to his thoughts, and he could feel the actual wounds inflicted by the lance and the nails, in his hands, his feet, and his side. (Huber. May, p. 1089.)

Many other like instances might be cited.

CHAPTER IV.

The manner in which the phenomenon of the Stigmata may be explained.

HAVING in the preceding chapter considered the mystical phenomenon of the Stigmata under its principal aspects, we are now qualified to form one, at least, probable opinion concerning its origin, its mode of action, and its course. One indispensable condition necessary for the reception of the Stigmata, a condition which invariably recurs in every fact of the kind which may be adduced, is an intense compassion for the sufferings of our Lord. The soul, while in the act of contemplating His Passion, receives from the Man of Sorrows an actual impression of Himself. Thus occupied, it would seem to be surrounded by an ocean of bitterness, and to be literally dissolving in ineffable sadness.

Now it is part of the very nature of the sentiment of compassion to transport a man out of himself, and to strip him of himself. He is thus actually invested, as it were, with his Beloved, and His image is graven upon him. The ecstatic state, and the visions which contemplations of this kind frequently engender, soon establish reciprocal communications between the soul and the object of its love. The soul penetrates deeper and deeper into the sufferings He has undergone. Her love and her compassion mutually increase each other, and the more she suffers, the more she becomes capable of suffering. Being thus ravished away, and forgetful of herself, she would fain appropriate still more the image of her Beloved. Her one prayer is to be permitted to suffer even as He has suffered. This thirst after suffering becomes intensified, and

nothing can suffice to quench it. Every drop
which falls out of that bitter chalice adds
fresh fuel to the flame, and stimulates without
assuaging the thirst which it creates.

Suffering, nevertheless, becomes the delight
of the soul, for her one desire is to be made,
by suffering, more like to Him whom she
loves. Inebriated with the burning wine
which she imbibes from her Saviour's Wounds,
she can find no rest until she beholds the
very image and impression of His sufferings
stamped upon the body which is her earthly
tabernacle; for by this means is wrought out
that perfect transformation into Christ, which
alone can satisfy her longings.

When this desire has been conceived, after
mature reflection, and has been freely and
openly expressed, it does sometimes happen
that the soul obtains its fulfilment by a pure
act of the grace of God, and so it comes to
pass that the actual Wounds of Jesus are set
upon the body. For the transformation of a
man into our Lord must necessarily be accomplished in the flesh, it being the spectacle of
the material sufferings of Jesus Christ which
has excited in the soul such tender compassion, a compassion which moves her to

6

sigh after physical pain. Now the sympathetic current which is thus established betwixt man and his Redeemer travels from the Body of Christ to that of His human adorer, and it works in the latter a material and sensible transformation.

The soul is the principle of life. Every impression, therefore, which it receives must be reproduced upon the body which it animates. For the soul is possessed of plastic power in an eminent degree, and during the term of this mortal life, it is united to the body by the closest possible ties. Hence it follows that nothing can take place in the soul, without being reflected upon the body. In accordance with this law, the soul may be said to have constructed, to a certain extent, the body which it inhabits; and every modification, which is wrought in the soul, will produce a similar metamorphosis in the body.

Supposing, therefore, the soul, in consequence of the compassion excited by the vision of our [Lord's sufferings, to become actually impressed with them; the act which thus assimilates it to Him is instantly reflected outwardly. The body shares, after a fashion of its own, in this marvellous assimilation, and thus the phenomenon of the Stigmata is produced.

This act, however, is accomplished in the soul by means of a very delicate process, for the object of the soul's affections appertains to the invisible world of spirits. The process, moreover, by which this act is reproduced on the body, is one of a most delicate nature also. For if, on the one hand, the body encloses the soul, on the other it may be said to be embraced and contained by the soul, for the soul far exceeds the body in magnitude.

Now the image of the suffering Saviour, having been once thus deeply graven in the very centre of the soul, assumes in visions an exterior form, which becomes perceptible to the senses by virtue of that bond which unites the soul to the body; and the impression of the Stigmata is made in the same way. It is the image conceived in the soul, and reproduced without in a sensible manner, which prints the wounds upon the body.

The channel of communication between the soul and the form, thus presented to its gaze upon these occasions, is vital heat. Having attained an extraordinary degree of intensity, it creates a very fire, and manifests itself by

luminous flames, which dart out from five
points, and direct their course towards the
corresponding corporal organs. The rays
emitted by this light are red, for red is the
colour that accompanies heat. But they are
white when the Stigmata does not appear
externally, remaining enclosed within the
human frame. Therefore it is evident that
light is the medium whereby that sacred type,
which is contained in the person of our Lord
Jesus Christ, is reflected and imprinted upon
the body of man.

Lucy of Narni affords an example of how
this applies, not only to the wounds of the
Stigmata, but to all the other signs as well.
One day, while she was praying before the
Altar of the Holy Cross, in the Dominican
church in her neighbourhood, all the bye-
standers beheld three rays issuing from the
Wounds in the side of the crucifix, which
illumined the countenance of the Saint.
Meanwhile, her head was surrounded throughout the whole of the Mass by a diadem of
light. Thus we may infer that the phenomena, accompanying the bestowal of the Stigmata, merely reproduce those which attend
the gift of illumination, but with this differ-

ence, that whereas illuminative power acts
upon life in its more exalted regions, the
imprint of the Stigmata is wrought in the
inferior regions of life, and in the blood which
is their motive source.

Thus we find that the crown traced out in
blood corresponds to the circlet of light which
rests over the brow of persons in ecstasy.
The bloody Sweat is represented by the luminous halo which surrounds their head. The
Wounds in the hands and feet find their coun-
terpart in the brilliant rays of light which
issue from the same members. The Wound in
the side corresponds to the light which ema-
nates from the heart, and the Scourging to
the halo which envelopes the entire person.

So that the faithful, sorrowing soul, which
would not be separated from Jesus in His
sufferings, is admitted to a participation of
His glory also, and this glory shines forth
externally in the members of the now transfigured body.

As we have already remarked, the soul
which operates all these changes constructs
its own dwelling-place, and that of the various
faculties which are attached to it. These
faculties are three in number, and they may

be said to reside in three distinct compartments.

The soul reserves the lowest storey for its own. It fixes its home in the heart. From the heart it diffuses itself into the organs of circulation. The second sphere contains the muscular system. The muscular system surrounds the spine, which is the main support of the whole fabric, and from thence its ramifications extend to the farthest extremities of the body. It extends, likewise, to the interior, along the prolongation of the spinal marrow to the annular protuberance, (at the base of the upper and lower brain,) where is found the centre of the motive life, of that life which is proper to it. The final, or third sphere, is apportioned to the brain, or cerebral system. Like the other two, this has its ramifications as well as its own centre.

So then the triple vitality which exists in man creates a triple organization. The first and highest region is set in communication with the lowest by means of the link formed by the middle sphere, which is placed betwixt them. The same description would apply to each separate centre. The centre of the brain is connected with the centre of the

heart by means of the centre of the intermediate system.

Consequently, when the soul, the architect
of the human body, receives the divine Stigmata, its impression will naturally be reproduced in those three regions of which we have
spoken. And so we shall find that the seraph
which appeared to St. Francis on Mount
Alverno had three pairs of wings. One pair
was attached to the head, which is the seat of
intellectual life and the organ of mental
power. The second pair of wings was attached
to the middle of the body, where reside the
organs of motion,—and these wings, be it
observed, were destined for the purpose of
flying. Lastly, the third pair veiled the
lower portions of the body, and symbolized
the life which is enclosed therein.

The soul, however, having been once marked
with the Stigmata in all its powers and
organs, tends towards an external manifesta-
tion of the impression made upon it. And
thus it comes to pass that the body exhibits
the sacred emblems in each one of the three
principal systems of which its nature consists.

The Stigmata are outwardly produced, upon
the head, by means of the bloody sweat and

the crown of thorns, corresponding to the two directions which the life of the brain pursues; the one reaching from the centre to within the circumference of the face, and the other stretching from right to left, and from the front to the back. The lower system, which maintains circulation, is stamped with the Wound in the heart, and as we have already seen, this wound will sometimes penetrate as far as the lungs, or to the region of the liver, which are both closely connected with this, the third, or inferior division of the human organism. Or again, the Stigmata will appear in the form of the Scourging, covering the whole of the skin with stripes and bruises. And finally, the wounds are manifested in the intermediate region, which governs the motive power, upon the hands and feet, or else they are imprinted upon the chest, in the form of a bleeding cross, at the spot where the muscles join and interlace each other.

It is not surprising that the image of the cross, when it is deeply impressed upon the soul, should be outwardly graven likewise upon the body. And then ensues that which befel Philip d'Aqueria, as we know, who never lost sight of our Lord's presence, but always beheld Him as suffering before him.

But in order to effect this complete impression of the Stigmata, a certain preparation is required on the part of man, in addition to the special disposition of the providence of God, and His own divine operation. None but He who created the soul and the body could work in them so great a transformation. He who set His own image and likeness upon them in the beginning alone can imprint upon them the seal of His suffering humanity also.

Now, if we analyze the dispositions which are requisite for effecting the phenomenon on man's part, we shall in the first place discover that great activity and great energy are needed in the vital forces, in order to enable them to receive and to retain for a long period those deep impressions, which we may presume must necessarily precede so great a change in the natural order of things as the Stigmata. Moreover, great pliability, mobility, and a very considerable degree of plastic power are indispensable in the bodily organs, so as to enable the soul to communicate its emotions promptly to the body, and to fix them thereon. The ordinary conditions of life cannot produce such results. Those conditions exact a certain amount of self-reliance and of firmness to render man capable of fulfilling the every-day purposes of existence. Now it is evident that if, in a general way, our emotions were so deep and so keen as to eventuate such startling results, nay, even to transform us, in a measure, into the actual objects of our affection, our entire life would be spent in continual migration from one form into another.

And although women, by reason of their natural constitution, are more disposed than men to receive impressions of the kind, nevertheless they too require a special preparation, which is supplied in this, as in all other cases, by an ascetic life. For the self-control which man acquires by means of abstinence and mortification exalts his higher powers, and detaches them from the material organs to which they are tied. And even matter itself becomes freer and purer under the influence of asceticism: it grows more impressionable. Thus we find that the Stigmata usually appears during Holy Week, or about that time. And this not merely because it is a season of sadness and of mourning in the ecclesiastical year, and the soul is therefore inclined to feelings of compassion, but because moreover, the fast of Lent, which precedes Holy Week, has given to the body that yielding and impressionable temper which is necessary for the development of so great a marvel.

Under favourable conditions such as these ecstasy has free play, and it would seem to take entire possession of the whole being of man. It enfolds him much in the same way as the mysterious slumber enfolded our first father, when God caused it to fall upon him before forming from his side a mother for the human race. In like manner, the new birth and bodily transformation, of which we are treating, takes place when, rapt in overflowing ecstasy, man, alone with his Creator, is absolutely removed from all contact with the things of earth.

As to the physiological process by means of which the phenomenon is brought about, our best authority on the subject is Brentano. He sets down what he had himself observed, in his Introduction to the Contemplations of Sister Catharine Emmerich of Dulmen. She received the crown of thorns

Catharine Emmerich of Dulmen.

when she was twenty-four years old, in the same manner as other ecstaticas have. At the age of twenty-three, when she was beseeching our Lord to let her share in His sufferings, she felt intense pain and great heat in her hands and feet. These sensations seemed to combine with those she already experienced in her heart, which she had won by her ardent prayers on former occasions. She, however, fancied her sufferings to be the effect of an habitual feverishness which had taken possession of her.

But not so. The fiat had gone forth. She was wounded, and the over-excitement produced by the wound displayed itself in burning and continuous fever. In this way the actual transformation which she was ultimately to undergo assumed its first faint outline. Later on she beheld, when in ecstasy, a young man resplendently bright, who made the usual sign of the cross over her with his right hand, and from that day forth she bore a mark resembling a cross on the epigastrium. Some weeks afterwards she saw the same apparition again, and this time she was offered a little cross, shaped like that described in the records of the Passion. She took it eagerly, and after pressing it fervently to her breast, returned it. After this an intense pain in her chest augmented day by day, and in attempting to discover the cause, she found that what appeared like a Latin cross, three inches long, was printed upon her breast bone. It was made apparent externally by a red mark upon the skin.

She did not, however, receive the complete Stigmata until the close of the year 1812. On the 29th of December, about three o'clock in the afternoon, she was in her little chamber. She was lying very ill upon her bed, but her arms were extended, and she was rapt in ecstasy. She was meditating upon the sufferings of our Lord, and begging to be permitted to suffer with Him. She repeated the Pater Noster five times, in honour of the Five Wounds, and while so doing her fervour was kindled afresh, and a glowing fire of love consumed her whole being.

She then saw a bright light descending towards her, and in it she distinguished the form of her crucified Saviour. His Five Wounds shone like five suns. Her heart was divided between conflicting feelings of grief and of joy, and when she looked upon the Five

Wounds her desire of suffering with our Lord grew more and more vehement. Triple rays of blood-red hue came from the hands and feet and side of the apparition. These rays terminated in the form of arrows, which pierced her hands and feet and her right side, excepting the threefold ray which issued from our Lord's side, which ended in the shape of an iron lance. The moment she was struck, drops of blood sprang from the wounds.

For a long time she remained unconscious, and when she recovered herself she knew not who had wounded her outstretched arms. She was astonished to find blood flowing from the palms of her hands, and she felt violent pain in her feet and in her side. The daughter of her hostess, a young girl who entered her room, saw her bleeding hands, and spoke of them to her mother.

The woman was alarmed, and anxiously inquired what had happened; but Catharine begged her not to speak of the matter.

After Catharine had received the Stigmata, she felt that a physical change had been wrought in her constitution. An alteration seemed to have taken place in the circulation of her blood. It took a new direction. A strong current bore it towards the wounds. Unable to explain herself in words, she was accustomed to say within herself, "These things are inexpressible."

It would often seem as though a burning stream issued from her heart, and after passing through her arms and legs, rushed impetuously towards the wounds. The wounds themselves caused her excruciating pain, and drops of blood fell from them. Very soon the veins which led to these spots became actually swollen. The Stigmata grew red and moist; the cross upon her breast yielded bright drops of blood; whilst the other cross raised a blister, which broke, discharging a colourless burning humour.[*]

This woman was not mistaken with regard to her bodily sensations. A real change in the circulation of the blood had taken place. In truth her heart might be said to have been divided into five portions. Each wound was in itself a lesser heart, and each was the source of a circulation proper to itself. Each and all were of course still tributaries of the natural heart, subordinate to it as to their

[*] "The Sorrowful Passion of our Lord Jesus Christ." Introduction.

centre and vital principle : but a far more
exalted Heart, even the Heart of our Lord
and Saviour Jesus Christ, was the loadstone
of their love, and from it it was that they
derived their chief impulse.

We may, then, conclude that in these cases
the ordinary course of the circulation of the
blood continues as usual. But when, at certain periods marked out by the ecclesiastical
year, that extraordinary mystical life, which
we are now considering, is developed in a
manner altogether singular, and one peculiar
to itself, we shall find that these abnormal
periphetic hearts cease to render to their
organic central source *all* that they have
drawn therefrom. They reserve a portion for
the supernatural Heart which now claims their
allegiance, and thus a new channel of circulation is opened; one similar in kind, however,
to that which exists under ordinary conditions, but which establishes a free current
between the mysterious stigmas and the
Sacred Heart of our Blessed Lord. The
Precious Blood contained in the Wounds of
Jesus flows into the wounds of those who
have been thus marked by Him, and its irresis-

tible influence acts upon the responsive tide which wells from their smitten members.

The supernatural union which welds all the faithful into one mystical body is commenced in the Holy Eucharist, and it is fully and absolutely completed in the person of those who receive upon their members the sacred imprints of the Passion. For thereby man enters into direct and immediate communication with the Blood which flows from the Adorable Heart of Christ,—from that riven Heart which once was emptied of all its Blood for the salvation of our race. The bearer of the miraculous imprints would seem borne away into the boundless current which unceasingly issues from, and returns again to, the Sacred Heart. And thus a new and more exalted life, a life kindled by the Spirit of God, lives and moves in the mystical Wounds of these living emblems of the Crucified. The flames of the sacrifice arise from five separate altars. These flames are red, for the burning heats of suffering and of pain give birth to them. And if at times they are extinguished to be replaced by a certain watery blood, which falls from the wounds, they would seem to have communicated to it a portion of their

7

fiery glow, for this liquid, as we have already
ascertained in several instances, scorches and
burns whatever it may chance to touch.

These upon whom our Lord has thus been
pleased to set His seal are they of whom S.
John speaks in the Apocalypse; they are of
the number of those " who follow the Lamb
whithersoever He goeth."   For how can they
be separated from Him to whom they have
been once for all united by the ties of blood?
Nourished by His most holy Flesh in the
Blessed Sacrament, He then transfuses His
Precious Blood into their veins.   His own
Heart beats in their heart, and the life He
breathes into them steeps the very marrow of
their bones.   The solemn sacrifice which is
daily celebrated upon the altar is perpetuated
in them in a bloody manner, thus forcibly
bringing to mind the act which was once consummated on Calvary.   And it is chiefly on
those days when the Church specially com-
memorates it that the miraculous wounds
open and bleed, as though to render the Passion and Death of our Saviour perpetually
present to the world.

CHAPTER V.

Of Mystical Plastic Power.
The Connection which exists between Phenomena of this kind and the Stigmata.

ANGELA OF PEACE—OSANNA OF MANTUA—THE HEART THE SEAT OF SUPERNATURAL EMOTION—CECILIA DE NOBILI —JANE MARY OF THE CROSS OF ROVEREDO—ISABELLA BARIS—CLARE OF MONTEFALCO—VERONICA GIULIANI— OF PLASTIC FORMATIONS IN THE BONE—BOLAND OF STRASSBURG.

WE meet with another phenomenon in the inferior regions of life, which is closely connected with the Stigmata. We refer to those plastic formations resulting sometimes from ecstasy. The objects which now completely possess and fill the soul become, so to speak, incarnate. That which the soul has interiorly assimilated to itself assumes actual shape and form in organic matter. Those external and visible crosses which sometimes appear upon the body, as, for example, in the case of Catharine Emmerich, partake of a transitional character. They furnish a connecting link between the phenomenon of the Stigmata and those which attend the operation of that plastic power which we are now to consider. Both kinds of phenomena, however, admit of the same explanation.

The Stigmata are produced by deep affections which have taken root in organs that have been purified and refined by an ascetic life. Affections such as these, likewise, give birth to plastic formations, as the result of their own abundant overflow. When our over-excited spirit can no longer contain itself it collects and clothes itself, to a certain extent, in unspoken words. Thus enclosed within itself, becoming its own object, it indulges in a sort of monologue, and converses with the echo of its own thoughts: or else, making use of articulate sounds, it becomes audible to other men through the medium of speech.

Now, the vital principle has, like the mind, its emotions and its various excitements. It acts, moreover, as the mind acts, but neces-sarily in a far grosser and more materialistic manner. Intertwined as it is with the body, and subjected, even as the body is subjected, to the conditions of matter, every motion it experiences will be externally manifested in accordance with material laws. The vital principle manifests its feelings by working such or such a change in the physical elements at its disposal, and by forming them into new shapes.

The whole body of man was thus formed in the very beginning, under the joint influence of the soul and of the vital principle. And it is preserved in the same way, the materials which compose its structure undergoing continual renovation. It need not therefore astonish us to find that when a new element, the divine element, comes to mingle with the other two, new and extraordinary formations should be produced. They are at once both the sign and the effect of a new and extraordinary state. They may be wrought in any portion of the human frame, but they usually appear in the central source of life, where all the vital powers are concentrated, namely, in the heart. And now it would seem as though man were gifted with a new heart, with a heart of a more exalted nature than before, that so fitting expression may be supplied to those sublime thoughts which will be infused into him from on high.

The heart is, as we know, the most compact

and the most material of all our bodily organs.
Restless, and self-consumed by its own cease-
less activity, it is forced to repair its organic
losses by the incessant creation of fresh matter. Now if, under the influence of mysticism,
it should become the organ of God's supernatural action, and the temple of His Spirit,
what wonder if the walls of the sanctuary be
covered with hieroglyphics, in which He is
pleased to symbolize the divine mysteries
enshrined within?

Angela of Peace. The close connection which exists
between phenomena of this kind and
those which characterize the Stigmata is clearly manifested by a
vision which Sister Angela of Peace had upon
a certain Friday. All at once her cell was
flooded with light, and our Lord appeared to
her in the midst of a choir of virgins. He
bore on His arm all the instruments of the
Passion, and He told her that He had at
length come to satisfy her desires. Then it
seemed to her as though the Child Jesus inflicted a wound upon her breast and heart,
and that He next proceeded to place within it
the instruments of the Passion which He held
in His hand. She underwent such intense

pain meanwhile that she fell down as one dead. Those who came to her assistance sent for her confessor, and he, suspecting what had taken place, commanded her, in virtue of holy obedience, to return to herself, and to relate what had happened to her.

She accordingly obeyed, but for a long while she was obliged to remain in bed, powerless to move in any way. She clearly perceived that the pains which extended over all her members sprang from her heart, and from the symbols of the Passion which had been set therein. One current of pain reached from the crown of thorns to her head, and another flowed from the nails to her hands and feet. The bitterness which issued from the sponge drenched her mouth with gall, and her shoulders and the surrounding parts felt the influence of the scourge.

Not long after the Holy Child appeared to her again in another vision. He said, "When, a little while ago, I brought thee the instruments of My Passion, thou desiredst so greatly to receive them that I placed them as they were, altogether, in thy heart. *Now* I am come to set them in order."

Whereupon He entered spiritually into her

heart, and arranged all the various instruments as it pleased Him. He set the cross in
the midst, over the point of the heart. The
crown of thorns was placed upon the upper
and more obtuse portion of it; the three nails
were set at the foot of the cross; the reed
and the sponge on the right side, and the
ladder on the left. The lance and the wound
in the heart were bestowed upon her at a
subsequent period. (Marchese, Oct. 5.)

**Osanna
of Mantua.**
This leads us to the considera-
tion of those plastic formations
which precede the Stigmata, as
in the case of Osanna of Mantua. Her heart
being still, to a certain degree, attached to the
things of earth, it seemed to her to be for
this cause somewhat livid. Our Lord took it
from her in a vision, and having purified it,
He restored it to her, bright and shining.
From that day forward she was so inflamed
with love for Him that for three years she
could only by dint of great effort succeed in
maintaining sufficient presence of mind at all.
She was rapt in almost continual ecstasy.
This state was succeeded by one of a very
different kind, which lasted seven years. During this time she endured trials of a most

painful nature. At the expiration of this period she began to pray earnestly for the tokens of the Passion, asking in the first place for the crown of thorns. Our Lord long delayed the fulfilment of her prayer, desiring by this means to increase her fervour. At length, at the end of two years He deigned to grant her request, and appeared to her wearing His crown of thorns. She prostrated herself at His feet, and as He placed the crown upon her head, so violent was the pain that she fainted away.

She received the sacred gift with gratitude and joy, but from the moment when it had been bestowed upon her she suffered from almost intolerable headaches. Her head was encircled with a visible ring or circle, which was often seen by those who lived with her, in spite of all the precautions she took to conceal it. It became swollen sometimes, and dark-coloured blood appeared to be circulating in it.

But the crown did not content her. She would share in all the Wounds inflicted upon her Beloved, and emboldened by what she had already obtained, she besought our Lord to give her still more. In the month of June,

in the year 1477, when she was thirty-two
years of age, she visited a holy maiden, called
Margaret Seraphina.   As the two friends
were speaking of the Apostle's words, "I
desire to be dissolved, that I might be with
Christ," Osanna was ravished out of herself.
During her ecstasy she again implored our
Lord to bestow His Five Wounds, and then,
finding that it was His will to defer this
favour, she entreated Him at least not to
refuse her the wound in the side.   She continued in prayer for three hours, urging the
same petition.   At length she beheld a
brilliant ray of light coming towards her left
side.   It entered into her body, striking and
piercing her with such force as to cause her
unutterable pain.   For a quarter of an hour
afterwards she was shaken by extraordinary
convulsive motions, which greatly astonished
Margaret, for she could in no way account for
all that had taken place.   When Osanna
recovered herself she attempted to conceal
the favour which had been bestowed upon
her; nevertheless, the room in which this
event occurred was shown long afterwards to
those interested in such matters.

Osanna was now satisfied, for she might

reasonably hope to obtain the complete fulfilment of her desire. She immediately began to pray for the other Wounds as well, and she succeeded in obtaining them after a year of fervent prayer. Our Lord appeared to her, surrounded by a bright light, and said to her, " Dost thou in very truth desire to bear My Wounds?" " I desire it more than words can say," she answered. " Beware, daughter," said our Lord, in return, "the pains thou seekest after are exceeding sharp, and greater than thou canst bear. It were better for thee to endure moderate suffering than to sink under new and grievous torture. Perchance thou mayest repent thee of thy prayer." " Nothing will prove too heavy a burden for my shoulders," answered Osanna, " if Thou but come to my help. Long since have I placed my hope in Thee; O fulfil Thy word." Then our Blessed Lord assured her of His succour, and burning rays came towards her, piercing her hands and feet. The intense anguish cast her to the ground, and she uttered a great cry. It was long before she recovered consciousness. The wounds were printed upon her hands, and even yet more deeply upon her feet. The edge of the wounds was swollen to such an extent that the nails might have been supposed to be forcing their way through them. They grew deeper on Wednesdays and Fridays, and in Holy Week, when they also became livid. At all other times they were visible to herself alone. An impenetrable veil concealed them from the gaze of man.

But her love was still unsatiated. The Wounds of her Beloved did not avail to suffice her: she desired to hold Him Himself within her heart. She begged Him to enter into it, that so she might always possess Him, for she could no longer live without His continual presence. And once more her prayer was heard. One day, after she had received Holy Communion, our Lord entered into her heart in the form of a crucifix, promising that He would never leave her. And His word was fulfilled, for from that time forth it always seemed to her as though a living form were enclosed in her heart. She felt movements in it as from side to side, and such motions as would be caused by arms extended and withdrawn. All this gave her such excruciating pain that she thought she must have died: nevertheless, her whole delight lay in these

sufferings. Finally, she besought our Lord to
let her feel all that He had experienced in
His Heart as He hung upon the cross. She
was again rapt in ecstasy, and it seemed to
her as though her heart were pierced with
a nail. The pain this caused her was so
extreme that she was forced to implore her
Divine Master several times to come to her
assistance.

However, she bore all her sufferings coura-
geously, although they often brought her to
the brink of the grave, according to the testimony of her confessor, upon several occasions.
One day he inquired how she was, and she
replied, with an angelic expression of countenance, " I live in great anguish, for the
whole region of the heart is swollen, from the
shoulder to the lower part of the chest, and
the pain, as well as the inflammation, extends
to my feet. My relative, Peregrina, rubs in a
certain ointment every day, and I say nothing
about it, lest she should divine the truth.
She has, however, remarked the inflammation
and the swelling, which spread like a band
from the chest to the shoulders, and which
are very painful to me." Her confessor then
asked her what was the nature of the pain she

felt in her heart. She answered, saying, "O my son, it would seem as though my heart were being cut in two, and then again sub-divided, like a pomegranate cut into four parts. Again I feel as though a knife were being drawn up and down the centre, which causes me most violent pain down one side. O good Jesus! how great is Thy goodness!"

Afterwards she received the crown of thorns as well. The skin inflamed round her head in the form of a circle, and projected about an inch in thickness, causing her intense suffering. It is not wonderful to find that in the end she became almost entirely unable to sleep. She was frequently very feverish, and often in the midst of conversation she would suddenly break off, and press her hand to her chest, being obliged to pause thus before resuming the thread of her discourse. At length it became impossible for her to meditate upon the mysteries of the Passion without an instantaneous inflammation of the heart. It appeared to be filled by some fiery body of considerable size, and as the pain spread over her entire person she became a prey to fever. (See her Life, by Fr. Sylv., of Ferrara, Milan, 1505; book iii. ch. 1, 2.)

Such, then, is love as it exists in great souls full of the Spirit of God. It has little in common with earthly love, which seeks after its own interest or pleasure; for, on the contrary, it thirsts for suffering only, and finally attains union with its object by means of heroic self-renunciation. Having once taken root in a strong and energetic soul, love like this developes a capacity for loving which pours in again upon its primary source, and there concentrates itself as in a furnace. A corresponding instinct impels the vital principle to gather itself up in the heart. The heart itself, agitated and uncontrollable under such a pressure of emotion, overflows on all sides, and it proceeds to express, in an unwonted manner indeed, but one still quite in accordance with its nature, the new and extraordinary impressions it has received. And it is in this way that it manifests that plastic power of which we have spoken. Now, the heart exhibits its activity in the blood, and through the blood. And it is in the blood, and more often still in the very heart itself, that the spiritual forms from which impressions are derived assume a compact and material shape.

No post mortem examination was made, either in the case of Angela or Osanna, in order to ascertain whether their physical organization had really been wrought upon as they believed it to have been. But others have been thus examined after death, and their heart has been found to bear the actual impression of the forms they had seen and felt.

Cecilia de Nobili. Cecilia de Nobili, a Poor Clare, bore, as we have already observed, the wound in the side, and it had penetrated so far as to reach the actual substance of the heart. After her death her heart was opened, and in it was found the likeness of two small scourges, marvellously composed of the membrane, interwoven with fibrous tissues. Rings, which were rendered distinctly visible by their dark colour, were attached to the lashes. (Huber. July, p. 1454.)

Jane Mary of the Cross, of Roveredo. Jane Mary of the Cross, of Roveredo, affords a similar example. In her case the wound had penetrated through the lungs to the heart, and the reed, the lance, and the sponge were all imprinted upon it. (Ibid., March, p. 766.)

After the death of Isabella Baris, a Theatine Nun, her heart was taken out and examined, in order to dis- **Isabella Baris.** cover the cause of the continual suffering she had endured in life. It was found to contain all the instruments of the Passion. (Sylos. p. ii. c. 10.) Sister Paul of S. Thomas, a Dominican, was accustomed to say that she carried the Crucified in her heart. After her death this was ascertained to be literally true, for the likeness of the dying Saviour was actually graven upon her heart. (Ibid.)

Once in a vision, Clare of Montefalco gave her heart to **Clare of Montefalco.** our Lord, that it might die upon His cross, and from that day forward she spent her whole life in continual meditation upon the Passion. After her death, which occurred in the year 1308, her Sisters in religion, thinking that something of a super-natural kind might have taken place, resolved to examine her heart. They first joined in prayer, and then one, more courageous than the rest, set resolutely to work. Having opened the thorax, the heart was found to be about as large as a child's head. It was removed from the cavity in the breast, and placed in a vessel upon the altar, for the Nuns could not make up their mind how to proceed. They therefore prayed again, and finally decided upon opening the heart. After some hesitation, Sister Frances struck the first blow with a knife, shedding a torrent of tears as she did so. She easily succeeded in cutting through the soft outer substance of the organ, but the internal part was harder, and offered some resistance. She then made a second incision, which divided the heart into equal halves, whereupon all the sisters, holding tapers, crowded round her, gazing with joy and veneration upon the mysteries of the Passion, which were arranged in due order upon the two panels of the heart.

In the midst, on the right side, was the figure of our crucified Redeemer. It measured a little over the length of a woman's thumb. The arms were outstretched, the head inclined, the right side was bare, the left was partly covered with a linen cloth stained with blood. At the feet, on the same side, (according to an extract from the acts, on the opposite side,) was the crown, which was composed of small fibres set with thorns. Near this were discernible three fibres, like in kind, fastened as threads would be, from which were suspended three pointed black nails, which were harder than the flesh to the touch. Two of the fibres, which were shorter than the third, were attached to still finer filaments. The lance was lower down, in an oblique position. The point was sharp, and of the colour of iron. It was so hard, moreover, that when Beranger, the Vicar-General, who was sent by the Bishop of Spoleto to investigate the matter, attempted to touch it, his finger was pricked as by a needle. Close to this lay a formless mass of red fibre, which was taken to represent the sponge. The scourge was to be seen upon the left side of the heart. It was composed of five flexible fibres, having many knots. The handle looked like wood, and was tied on with a small knot. The lashes, which were dyed purple with blood, were detached from the flesh, and thus they may be seen to this day at her tomb. Beside these stood the pillar, which seemed to be encircled with cords dyed in blood.

The bishop instituted a most careful inquiry concerning the facts. All the instruments of the Passion were removed. Some were sent to the Pope, in order to the beatification of

the Saint, and the rest were preserved at her
tomb. Most interesting details relating to
the occurrence are to be found in the Life of
Blessed Clare of Montefalco, written by
Béranger Moscomo and Curtius. It was compiled partly from manuscripts preserved in
her convent, and partly from the acts of her
beatification.

Veronica Giuliani. But the most remarkable instance of this kind is to be found
in the Life of Veronica Giuliani.
The phenomenon we are now considering was
perhaps never produced in so perfect a manner, nor has its operation ever been more
carefully observed than in her case. We
have already had occasion, moreover, to notice
the scrupulous attention which the Saint herself bestowed upon facts of this nature.

On Holy Saturday, in the year 1727, she
had disclosed to her confessor, under holy
obedience, that she bore divers signs and
figures in her heart. He then, after having
deliberated concerning what she had made
known to him, very prudently resolved to
procure an authentic document, which would
enable him fully to ascertain the truth of the
matter after her death. He therefore com-

manded her once more, in virtue of obedience,
to depict the state of her heart on paper, just
as she had described it to him by word of
mouth. She complied with his desire, but
being unable to draw herself, she begged two
of her sisters in religion, Florida Ceoli and M.
Magdalen Boscami, to help her in the execution of the task. She did not, however, speak
of it as a serious matter, but sought rather to
represent the whole as a mere fancy of her
own. Accordingly, a piece of red paper was
cut into the shape of a heart, then the following emblems were cut out of white paper,
under her direction, and pasted upon it.

A tall Latin cross was set in the midst,
over the point of the heart; on the left the
crown of thorns was placed, and over the top,
above the cross, a banner, the staff whereof
was composed of two separate pieces. She
directed the upper portion to be cut out of
dark red paper. Above this again rose a
flame of the same hue, and below it was a
hammer, a pair of pincers, a lance, and the
reed full length. To the right of the cross,
on the upper part, was our Lord's seamless
robe, a second flame, a chalice, two wounds
united, the pillar, three nails, the scourge,

and lastly, beneath the cross itself, seven
swords with their points turned inwards.
Veronica then took a pen, and drew a line
from the chalice to the cross, which united all
the twenty-four ensigns together. She then
proceeded to trace in ink eight Roman capitals
in several places, and one other letter in a
running hand. On the top of the cross she
set C, which, according to her interpretation,
stood for Charity; on the left arm was an O,
for Obedience; on the right U, for Humility;
and in the midst FF, Faith and Fidelity.
On the two divisions of the banner she put J
above and M beneath, for Jesus and Mary.
At the foot of the cross, on either side, PP,
symbolizing Passion and Patience; and
lastly, she set V below the points of the seven
swords, for Voluntas, the will of God. The
two flames represented the love of God and of
our neighbour, and the two wounds those
which she had herself received on Christmas
night.

The diagram was completed by Pentecost,
and was given to F. Guelfi, her confessor, by
the Saint three days before the fit of apoplexy
which nearly caused her death. He signed
the paper, and after sealing it, sent it to the

bishop. At a later date, during the course of the process for her beatification, when the seal and the signature were submitted to him, he acknowledged them for his own. A copy of the design, made by Sister Ceoli, is still preserved in the convent.

After Veronica's death, her heart, by command of the bishop, was opened in due form by John Francis Gentili, a professional surgeon, and by J. F. Bordiga, a physician. The operation was performed in the presence of the governor, Torrigiani, of the chancellor, Fabbri, of two priors, Pesecci and Gellini, and two doctors, Falconi and Giannini; her confessor, Guelfi, the painter Luc Antonio Angelucci, and several Nuns assisting also.

The cross, bearing the letter C, was found to be very distinctly marked, as well as the crown of thorns, the two flames, the seven swords in a fan-like position, the letters V and P, the lance and the reed cross-wise, the flag-staff in two parts, and the letters J and M, and a nail of the kind usually represented. The bishop did not think it necessary to make a deeper incision into the right side of the heart. Thirty-four hours had elapsed since the Saint's death, and he entertained fears for its preservation. He was also anxious to spare the feelings of the Sisters who were present as much as possible. (See her Life, p. 124, and the Acts of the Process for her Beatification, which were drawn up two months after her death.) The same thing befel Margaret of Citta di Castello.

Boland
of
Strasburg.

This plastic power is not confined to the more pliable portions of the body, but it extends to the bone likewise. Cantinpré, in his first book, "Des Abeilles," ch. 25, relates the following fact as one which he himself was witness to. Boland, the Prior of the Dominicans at Strasburg, was continually in the habit of making the sign of the cross upon his breast with his thumb. He had occasion to go to Mayence, where he was attacked by the malady of which he died, and he was buried in that city with the Friars Minor. The Dominicans at Strasburg wished to have his body, but the Friars were anxious to retain it. After a lapse of some years, however, the Convent at Mayence was removed elsewhere, and the Dominicans were at length able to translate the remains to Strasburg.

When they washed the bones they found a cross, perfect in form, imprinted upon the bone of the thorax, precisely at the junction of the ribs. It seemed to cover the heart as with a shield. Cantinpré, who travelled forty miles in order to witness this marvel, tells us that he himself saw the cross, which was moulded in relief, of the very substance of the bone, in the middle of the thorax. The summit and the arms were of the same length, but the plinth was longer. The upper portions terminated in lilies, but the foot of the cross was pointed, like one intended to be sunk into some socket. In another document cited by Bzovius, in the year 1237, it is added that the cross was blue. John of Yepes died in 1591, and one year after his body was discovered perfectly intact and without blemish of any kind ; it exhaled, moreover, a delicious perfume. It was laid, in the presence of a great concourse of people, in the Carmelite convent at Segovia. Wonderful representations of our Lord, of the Blessed Virgin, and of angels and saints, were to be seen traced upon every limb. But these did not appear alike to every one, nor did each one behold them altogether. Some failed to see anything, and others saw them, sometimes in one way, and sometimes in another. In this case, therefore, a subjective element enters into the question concerning the reality of the appearances, and the certainty of the fact cannot be incontestably established.

The bishop of the diocese, Vigilis de Quinone, states, it is true, that a great number of individuals saw these signs, and their existence has been confirmed by most trustworthy witnesses. It was also attested in due form in the process. Nevertheless it remains difficult in cases of this kind to distinguish between the actual fact and what may have been merely the effect of imagination. (Paradisus Carmeletici decoris, p. 435.)

CHAPTER VI.

Extasy Considered in the Organs of Motion.

The Mystic Stations—This Phenomenon how joined
with that of the Stigmata—Lucy de Narni—How
it is produced in one part only, or in a complete
manner—Saint Colette—Agnes of Jesus—Jane of
Jesus Mary.

EXTASY takes hold of the whole man.
But, though man is only a single person, he has in this unity several different regions, in each of which he exercises
a special manner of action. So also it is
with the Spirit from on high in His produc-
tion of an extasy. The Spirit is always the
same, but as He wills He takes hold of sometimes one, sometimes another of these various
regions in man, and produces thus particular
phenomena. We have seen how, when He
subjects to His action the vital forces, He
raises them above themselves, and gives them
a greater plasticity, making them to produce
in the organism extraordinary forms. It is
thus that the phenomena of stigmatization
are manifested in all their degrees.

Now, the two extreme regions in man, which represent in a special manner the two first Persons of the Trinity, find their point of union in this intermediate region, which presides over the motions of the body. When extasy has laid hold principally either of the mind or of the inferior region of a man, the organs of motion are ordinarily tied, so that visions, and stigmatization too in part, take place during a calm and motionless extasy. But it happens sometimes that the Divine Spirit takes possession of this intermediate region, and works in it an extraordinary increase of activity. Those organs, which in the two first forms of extasy were tied, are, on the contrary, in this case elevated to a much higher power. Their movements, directed by the will in a supernatural state of exaltation, pass beyond their ordinary and natural limits, and so an extasy in movement succeeds to a motionless extasy.

Extasy in motion holds a middle place between extasy of mind, which produces visions, and plastic extasy, which gives birth to the stigmata. There are in it three distinct degrees, answering to the three aspects of the organs of motion. In the first degree may be classed all those phenomena entitled mystic stations. In the second degree are comprised all extasies in which an action is wrought at a distance, whether the action goes from or comes to the centre of motion. The third degree consists of extasies in which a man walks in the air, or his body is elevated, or he flies. We shall here study the mystic stations.

Extasy in motion answers, in the order of grace, to somnambulism in the order of nature. **Mystic Stations.** When man walks whilst awake, the mind holds the rudder, and directs from above the motion made to a fixed and certain end. But when a somnambulist walks in sleep, the instinct of the lower regions in man's life takes the place of the intelligence, clouded over by sleep, and directs the organs of motion with that assured certainty which is characteristic of every natural instinct. In extatic motion the Spirit of God takes the place of the mind of man. The mind during the time of the extasy is subjected to the Spirit, something in the same way as instinct is ordinarily to the mind, with this difference, that the subjection of instinct, in the inferior,

life of man, to the mind, is necessary and
continual, whereas the subjection of the mind
in extasy is voluntary and for a time only.
The Divine Spirit, whilst it takes possession
of the power of man, exercises it in its fashion
by producing motions, which his will within
gives consent to, and which his organs exe-
cute without. A new world of action is thus
opened, marked out by the Spirit of God, just
as the circle of a man's ordinary waking life is
contained within the sphere of his own mind;
whereas, whilst he is asleep he reposes in the
bosom of nature, or in the lower region of his
organic life, subject exclusively to the in-
fluences of nature.

In the domain of mind and of nature, when
an important end is to be attained, and there
are considerable means of carrying it out,
the actions performed take an epic or drama-
tic form, and the whole put together form
a sort of sublime poem. Just so is it also
in the domain of grace. Here when the
spirit of God and of man are at union in
an action common to both, from their con-
certed operations knit together, there is
formed a glorious and striking drama. But
the most exalted object which can be pro-

posed to the mind of man when taken possession of by the Spirit of God is our Lord Himself, accomplishing the work of redemption
for which He came on earth, and mounting
the road that leads to Golgotha. No spectacle strikes the mind so deeply with tender
emotions as the scenes of the Passion. As
when two chords are tuned to the same tone
the vibration of the one sets the other in like
movement, so the sufferings of our Lord, con-
templated by a loving and enraptured soul,
set in motion the affections of the soul that
gazes on them, and produce in her the same
sentiments which our Lord Himself experienced. It is no longer a simple meditation. It is a living reproduction of the
Saviour's Passion in all its acts and all its
circumstances. Just indeed as the plaints
torn from the heart by sympathetic compassion form a sort of melodious lament,
so the reproduction of the scenes of sorrow of
the Saviour's Passion make up a sublime
drama, at which it is impossible to assist
without deepest emotion.

By all that has been just said
it is easy to see the relation   Lucy Narni,
between this phenomenon and that of stig-

matization. An example of such relation is
given us in the stigmatization of Lucy Narni.
On February 4th, 1496, when she was in
Choir with twenty-five Nuns of the same Convent, she fell into an extasy, and remained
motionless for half an hour. Then, as she
sent forth a deep plaintive cry, they understood that she was making with our Saviour
the Stations of His Passion. They saw that
she suffered the pains our Lord and His
Mother endured when parting, and that our
Saviour felt at the desertion of His disciples
and the treachery of Judas, she herself wishing
to bear them instead of Him. She followed
our Lord to the pillar, and lost in anguish,
asked to receive herself the blows which
were inflicted upon Him. Heart-broken,
she viewed the crowning of thorns, in com-
pany with Mary, with Magdalene, and S.
John. She heard the wrongful sentence of
Pilate, and accompanied the funeral procession towards Calvary. She followed close on
the steps of our Saviour, and took gladly on
her shoulders the cross, in place of Simon the
Cyrenean. Then, bending beneath the dreadful burden, she fell to the ground, worn out
with weariness and anguish. Coming again

to herself, she dragged on as well as she could, following in the track of the Saviour, crying, " O my Lord, I see Thee fastened to the cross. I wish to be fastened to it with Thee. Let me have my part in Thy sufferings, and a share in Thy sacred wounds."

Sister Diambræ, approaching the extatic, saw the muscles of her arms contracted convulsively and the bones dislocated. She asked her what was the matter with her arms, to which Lucy answered that they seemed asleep. Soon, however, the cramps increased to such an extent that her arms grew stiff, and became cold as ice; and her pulse faded to almost nothing. This lasted till tierce, when she went to communicate with the others. So soon, however, as she got back to her cell, Sister Diambræ noticed that in the palm of her hand was a spot of the appearance of blood, and during the following week the Five Wounds of our Lord were completely formed in her body.

Lucy de Narni is celebrated for the severity of the examination to which her stigmatization was subjected. As soon as the bishop heard of it he forbad the stigmata to be touched, or any cure of them to be attempted.

9

But as they remained ever fresh, and without suppuration, only bleeding more abundantly on Wednesdays and Fridays, he allowed them to be bandaged, and some remedies to be employed, but all in vain. An inquest into this affair was set on foot by Pope Alexander VI., the committee being composed of the Grand Inquisitor, the Bishop of Narni, the Prior of Viterbo, several canons, and the physician, Al. Gentiari. These, after a strict examination, pronounced the thing to be supernatural.

However, people did not cease their talk. Every one had his word and his own opinion. Lucy was treated as a hypocrite, and the thing made such a noise that Duke Hercules of Este begged the Pope to send Lucy to him at Ferrara. He there charged four of the principal physicians of Ferrara, and three others besides, *omni exceptione majores*, as the author of S. Lucy's Life expresses it, together with two bishops and the Archbishop of Milan, to proceed to an exact inquest of the matter. They acquitted themselves conscientiously of their task, and confirmed the judgment of the first commission.

But even this was not found sufficient.

Alexander VI. therefore sent his own physician, Bernard de Recanati, one of the most famous physicians of the time, and two bishops, to proceed to a new inquisition into the matter. Bernard had a glove made that no one could open but himself, and he put it on the hand of Lucy, fastened it, and sealed it with his seal. He left it on nine days. If the wound had been natural it would have begun during that time to suppurate; but on taking it off the wound was found just as fresh and red as before. This third commission then decided as the others had done, and the calumny was put to silence. Bosio, in his book on Signs, affirms that he had himself seen the acts of this last inquisition at Rome.

The phenomena of stigmatization are not always complete in **S. Colette.** the same individual. Some receive the wounds in the feet only, or the hands, head, or heart only. It is the same with the phenomenon of which we are now treating. The sacred drama of our Saviour's Passion is not always reproduced in its entirety in extatics, especially with those who are but beginners in the mystical life. S. Colette, who, during her extasies, filled all the house with an agreeable odour, considering one day, during a rapture, the Passion of the Saviour, her face swelled up as if it had been struck with many blows, seeming only to be of skin and bone. Her nose seemed all beaten out of shape. When she had ended her meditation, her face, as the Sisters beheld her, resumed its former natural appearance. The swelling went away, and her nose took its old shape. It is plain S. Colette bore in her countenance the marks of the evil treatment our Lord received from the soldiers and His executioners.

With others are reproduced the Agony of our Lord in the Garden of Olives, or the scourging, or some other scene of the Passion. When, however, all the scenes succeed each other, then only it is that the entire drama is represented, with all the motives and circumstances that compose it. This drama is pictured forth in a manner more or less vivid, and is beheld by the spectators with an emotion more or less profound, according to the particular conditions of the person in whom it is reproduced.

A great number of examples confirm all that has just been said. Let us select the most striking,

Agnes of Jesus.

following the order of the interest they inspire. Agnes of Jesus had first the crown of thorns, then pains in the heart, then in the hands and feet, in which were first manifested small blood-coloured crosses. She was, after this, led to Calvary to assist at the crucifixion, and then the stigmata were completely formed on her body.

A short while after her profession an Angel appeared to her, and said, " Agnes, prepare to suffer as much as any creature has ever suffered." She contented herself with answering, " Do not abandon me when what you announce shall come to me." That very evening, when she was in bed, her chamber was of a sudden filled with a glorious light, in the midst of which was seen Jesus Crucified, covered with wounds and inundated with Blood. At this spectacle it seemed as if she herself were also stretched on a cross, and nailed through the hands and feet. The agony she endured was such that she filled the chamber with loud cries, and the Sisters, running in, found her hands stretched out,

and her feet placed one over the other, and as
it were nailed to a cross. When she saw the
Sisters she said to them, "O, my dear Sisters, pray for me, for I cannot endure more."
They called her confessor, fearing she might
die without the sacraments of the Church.
Agnes made her confession in floods of tears,
and received the Viaticum, after which she
fell into an extasy, shedding around her, as
usual, a delicious perfume. The Blessed
Virgin appeared to her and comforted her,
but only for a few instants.

The heavenly message gave her courage for
new sufferings. These came very shortly,
and continued three days, after which they
became less, and were only in her side, her
hands, and feet, so that she was for a long
time unable to walk.

At the end of a year she was seized, whilst
in the garden of the Monastery, with such
violent pains that she fell on the ground
backwards. There the Sisters found her,
with her arms stretched out like one dead.
They took her up and carried her to her cell,
where she remained for three hours without
any sign of life. When she came to herself
she was brought to the Prioress. The pain

soon returned, and she was heard to cry with a tenderness indescribable, " O Love, how powerful Thou art ! O Love, mighty, irresistible ! Dear Sister, I have no longer a heart; Love has taken it away. I cannot speak myself; it is Love speaks by my mouth. Let us love this divine Love that so tenderly loves us." Then, turning to the crucifix, she said, " O Lord, my sweet Love ! I desire to suffer to the end of my life." Perceiving her confessor, she said, " Father, give your child what she wants." He heard her confession, and gave her Holy Communion. She then was ravished for an hour. When she came to herself her confessor asked her where she had been. She answered, " I come, Father, from the palace of love." " Where is it ?" he said. " On Calvary," she replied. " There I saw my Saviour carrying His heavy cross all alone. He told me I should carry mine without any mixture of comfort."

The cramps soon returned. Her body was stretched out by an invisible force, and her hands drawn with violence. Her feet were placed one over the other, and all her limbs were shook with violent agitation. The joints of her bones were heard to crack, and within

her breast was heard a singular sound, as
if her heart was being torn out. During
this time she did nothing but beseech God
for patience and strength, exhorting those
round her to love our Lord. She then had a
new extasy, followed by new pains, which
became so cruel that they administered to her
the sacraments of the dying. During this
time she received some visions that comforted her.

The following day the invisible messenger
appeared to her anew, and asked her if
she were willing to suffer still more for the
sins of the world. She answered, "Yes;"
and in about an hour's time her sufferings
returned more dreadful than before, so that
all present were amazed that she could live
on. She asked for a crucifix, that was near
her, but before it was given, it was seen
to come to her of itself, as by a magnetic
attraction. The Sisters expected her to die
every minute, but a voice told her she should
live to the following day. They put some
sugared wine into her mouth to refresh her,
but it tasted to her like vinegar and gall.
The following day was a Friday, and then

was enacted the last scene of this terrible drama.

As her confessor exhorted her to patience, she assured him that amidst her greatest sufferings God had always accorded her the grace of entire resignation to His holy will. Towards eleven o'clock the signs of approaching death became apparent, and she was told to be ready. She said that if it were God's will she should die, it would be highly agreeable to her; but she doubted of it. Meanwhile her confessor began the prayers of the agonizing, and she, perfectly resigned, began the death struggle. The Sisters, who were at table, were called to her bedside to recite the litanies. Death pursued his work, and Agnes remained without motion. The Sisters then all hasted to the Choir and took the discipline, to obtain from God that she might live. Her confessor remained alone with her, when she opened her eyes, and cried out aloud, "I am come back." She recounted the visions she had had. The Sisters returned, and were amazed and transported with joy to find their dear Sister recovered. They tenderly embraced her, and thanked God for her cure.

This took place in the month of February, 1626. She began to eat, for she had scarce touched anything for six weeks, and she was able to be present at compline. Her life has been written in French by a priest at Auvergne, from the MSS. of Prior Bianchi, Provincial of Boyre, and those of the Archpriest Martinon, and her confessors, Ponassier and Ferèsse.

An example not less striking is that of Jane of Jesus-Mary, at Burgos. What renders this case more valuable is, that the circumstances, which so interest this matter, have been related in her life with minute detail by Francis d'Aymayugo, whereas that of Agnes only gives a general summary. Jane, widowed in 1622, took the habit in the Convent of S. Clare at Burgos, in 1626, after having lived in the world sixty years. She began her new life with terrible and countless mortifications. She fulfilled all the rules of the Monastery, and added over and above her old pious practices. One of these, which was her darling devotion, was meditating on the bitter Passion of the Saviour. Even before this the drama of blood on Calvary had been reproduced in her, but in the silence of the cloister it reached the climax of its perfection. The Abbess, who was in the secret, shut her up in her cell every Thursday evening, that she might not be disturbed, and did not open the cell till six on Friday evening, for then she had finished her exercise. Spite of all precautions, the curiosity of the other Sisters, quickened by the mystery which was sought to be concealed, found means of satisfying itself. Indeed, they ended by getting into her cell itself. This was the more easy, as during her extasies she was quite unconscious of their presence. Here, then, is the evidence they gave on oath when an examination was made. And they declared they were eye-witnesses to all the things of which they gave testimony, having followed her movements step by step.

On Thursday evening she began ordinarily by examining her conscience, and asking pardon of God for all her sins. Then she entered into the upper room, where the Last Supper took place. The Sisters having found her sitting in extasy, saw her rise, and walk on her knees in the cell, stopping here and there, and bowing as before some man sitting down. It was easy to perceive that she was occupied in the washing of the feet. She then rose, sang some hymns of thanksgiving, and began walking again. She was evidently following our Lord to the Garden of Olives. Arrived there, she meditated on our Lord's Agony, and shared in His sadness and His anguish. She remained from eight to eleven plunged in deep meditation. Part of that time she stood, and part she passed prostrate on the ground. There was seen on her countenance a trouble ever increasing. Her eyes were bathed in tears. Her distress became ever greater, and the sorrow of her soul more piercing. When her emotion was at its full a sweat of blood poured from her body so abundant that its drops fell on the ground.

About eleven o'clock the troops brought by Judas to apprehend our Saviour attracted her attention. The Sisters saw her rise and walk. They saw her cast on the ground with great violence, but throughout she preserved on her face a remarkable expression of majesty and loving-kindness. She was representing our Lord when seized by the soldiers. Then she considered Him as betrayed by Judas, loaded with chains, beaten, outraged, led prisoner by a maddened soldiery. She followed Him as He passed on, and regarded the blood-stained track of His feet. She saw Him fall on the road, His face all bruised, and her own countenance became black and blue. The blood gathered under her nails, and her arms and hands showed marks of violence, as though they had been injured by cords and chains bound exceedingly tight.

About one in the morning she saw the Divine Prisoner in the hall of Annas, His head and feet naked, the eyes down-dropped towards the ground, and His features bearing the print of the humility of heaven. She heard the high-priest question Him concerning His doctrine and His disciples, and saw the blow given to the Saviour by one of the servants of the high-priest, a blow so violent that He fell to the ground, and the Blood gushed from His mouth. One of the cheeks of the extatic became black and swelled, as if she had herself received the blow. She followed Jesus to the hall of Caiphas, sharing in all the ill-treatment He received. She heard with horror Peter's denial of his Lord; and the rest of the night she passed in a corner of her cell, as though she had herself been plunged into a dungeon.

On Friday, about four in the morning, Jane rose and walked in her cell from one place to another, so that it was seen she was being led before the judgment-seat of Pilate and Herod. When she saw our Saviour condemned to be scourged her heart was torn with anguish. She saw in spirit the executioners come down in great number into the porticoes of the judgment-hall, where a crowd of people was assembled. They ordered our Lord to take off His clothing, and they themselves tore them off Him. About eight o'clock it was when she received the scourging. Her face became quite blue, and her features drawn, like those of one dead. She crossed her hands and bowed herself, as though attached to a low pillar. She remained a long time like that. Then her countenance, which had been pale as death, became troubled in a pitiable manner, so that it was seen that the scourging then occupied the attention of her soul.

Towards nine o'clock she arrived at the crowning with thorns, considering the curse pronounced by God on the earth, a curse

truly fulfilled notably in the person of our
Saviour. At the end of the scourging she
had fallen fainting on the ground. She rose
slowly and trembling, sat on the ground, shut
her eyes, and crossed her arms. Then from
her head began to flow little tricklets of blood.
It seemed, too, as if she were buffeted on the
cheeks, for her face, aforetime pale, became
swelled and bloody, so as to be pitiable to
look at. The Sisters judged by all these
things that the crowning with thorns was
thus being reproduced in her.

From ten till midday she followed her
Beloved, with all the people, till He ascended
Mount Calvary, and her grief was redoubled
at beholding that of the holy Virgin when she
met her Son on the road. At the beginning
of her meditation she had unfastened an iron
cross from the wall, weighing thirty-three
pounds, which is still preserved in the Convent. She put it on her shoulders, and
walked thus with it on her knees through the
cell. When she met the Blessed Virgin wait-
ing for her Son, she stopped awhile, and
addressed her with words so sweet and tender
as to fill all the Sisters with deep emotion.
When she had taken leave of the Blessed

Virgin, she walked on after the Saviour. From midday till one o'clock she meditated on the crucifixion. Leaving the iron cross, she took one of wood, made expressly for her, to the measure of her height. This she laid on the ground, and placed herself on it, and seemed verily to be nailed to it.

After some instants the Sisters saw the cross, with Jane on it, lifted up into the air, where it remained by a miracle, not touching the ground. There flowed streams of blood from her head, her hands, her feet, and her side. From the cross she looked down from time to time on the Blessed Virgin, and she considered how this Mother of Sorrows was in heart crucified with her Son, by the distressing sorrows which she endured, suffering in an unseen mode what He suffered visibly. The Nuns then heard her pray for all those that had been recommended to her, whether living or dead. At about three o'clock she cried with a loud and lamentable voice, "My God, my God, why hast Thou forsaken me;" after which her mouth and features contracted as if she had tasted some bitter draught.

She passed on then to consider the death of our Saviour, asking to die with Him. When the moment came that He commended His soul into His Father's hands, she commended hers with His, and after pronouncing the words, "*All is consummated,*" she bowed her head, as though she had no strength to breathe any longer. She fell then from the cross to the ground, the cross still remaining as before in mid-air. A short while after she raised herself on her knees, and turned towards the cross. She appeared to offer her veil to some one, by which the Sisters understood that she presented it to the Blessed Virgin, to wrap it round the body of her Son for burial. All this time she remained recollected, but weeping bitterly, and she addressed some affectionate words to the Blessed Virgin. This lasted till five or six in the evening.

She then came out of her extasy. It was the hour when the Abbess was accustomed to come. She had the blood washed away that had been shed during the extasy, and Jane then resumed her ordinary life. During all this moving scene the Sisters were astonished at the singular dignity and modesty of all her gestures and the positions she took. But at each step her bones made a sound that

10

could be heard some way off. During all the time of this holy exercise there were two lights burning on the altar in Jane's cell. It happened once that the Abbess and Sisters put them out, and fastening the door, went away; but when they returned the lights were burning again. When Jane came out of her extasy she could on the very same night come to matins, although she had lost such a quantity of blood.

This marvel continued twenty whole years, being renewed regularly every week. Even in 1617, the public notary at Burgos had drawn up a regular juridical statement of the facts at the request of the barefooted Clares, and renders testimony of what he had seen. He first cites the request, three times made, of the Clares; he then names the street, the house, and chamber in which he found Jane, the witnesses he met there, and those he carried with him. Among other things, he mentions having seen a quantity of blood coming out of the corners of the eyes on Friday morning during the crowning with thorns. Part of this blood flowed in little drops like a dew, hanging awhile on the lashes, and then falling in large drops over

the face. He also saw a quantity of blood
come from her mouth and nose, so that her
neckerchief was steeped with it. This blood,
however, was not so red, being mixed with
saliva and mucous matter. She afterwards
sat on her heels, and whilst in that position
made four respectful inclinations; then she
walked on her knees, and dragged herself
to the foot of a cross which was there, and
during that time her skull cracked with a
frightful noise. Then she took the cross on
her shoulders, and carried it till a quarter
past twelve at noon; then she fell into a faint
which lasted three hours. She took the cross
with a groan, and unfastened it from the wall.
The cross remained afterwards in the air
without support, not propped up by Jane
with her knees. To assure himself of this,
one of those present took a light, and approached the cross, so that he was convinced
the cross only just touched the ground, un-
supported in any way, so that it could not so
stand but by a miracle. He says that between two and four o'clock she remained in
extasy, fastened to this cross; that her confessor blew her and the cross about with his
breath several times; and that she went

about like a light leaf in the air. Later on she came down to the ground, and leaned her head on her right hand. He went to her to see what she was doing, and, examining her face, found it perfectly clear of blood; only a few drops remaining in the right nostril. She then fell again into an extasy, and her countenance shone so that the light could be perceived at the door of the cell outside.

About five o'clock she again went about the cell without the cross, as she had done in the morning. She made four inclinations profoundly, and between five and six o'clock she came out of her extasy with a deep sigh, saying, "O my Jesus." These were the only words she had pronounced since morning; the rest had been only sighs or groans. During all this time she had given no sign of consciousness, whether on being called or touched, or when her pulse was being felt.

At the age of seventy, as the loss of so much blood every Friday exhausted her strength extremely, her superiors commanded her, in virtue of holy obedience, to ask of God to close her wounds. She obeyed. She

prostrated herself before a picture of the
Ecce Homo, and God graciously heard her
prayer. The following morning, as she prepared for Communion, she felt within her
a great emotion; she looked at her hands,
and the wounds were gone. The same thing
had happened in the other wounds of her
body. From that moment she wore the
scars only.

CHAPTER VII.

Mystic Stations.—Continued.

Veronica Juliani—Jane de Carniolo.

TO the examples already cited may be
added the case of Veronica Juliani.
Under the direction of a clever and discreet man the phenomena were developed
in all their forms, were examined attentively,
and the result of the observations was em-
bodied in a clear authentic statement.

As the symptoms of her extraordinary state
became more and more manifested, Eustochi,

the Bishop of the diocese, wished to be able
to have a clear conviction as to their nature.
He therefore got Father Crivelli, a Jesuit of
great reputation as a guide of souls, to come
in 1714 from Florence. He let him know all
that had occurred, and then, removing the
ordinary confessor of the Convent, he named
him confessor extraordinary, and enjoined
him to remain two months in the Convent for
the purpose of proving Veronica.

The Father then obeyed, and, as is usual in
the like circumstances, he first got the Saint
to make a general confession. He then, from
what he had learned from her, or from the
other Sisters, determined to bring the affair
to a decisive proof. For this purpose he
caused her one morning to come to the confessional, and commanded her at once to put
herself in prayer, telling her to ask God to
reveal to her what he commanded her in
his own heart. Veronica consented, and
began to pray. Whilst she was thus praying,
Crivelli addressed to her the following five
commands. 1. That the wound of the side,
which was closed, should open and bleed
again, like those of the feet and hands. 2.
That it should remain open as long as he

willed it. 3. That it should close in his presence, and in that of any others he should please to have present. 4. That she should suffer in a visible manner, when he should judge convenient, all the pains of the Passion. 5. That, after suffering the crucifixion, stretched on her bed, she should afterwards suffer in mid-air erect, by his order, before him and before such as he should choose to admit.

After having given these commands in his own mind, he left her some time in prayer, and then inquired if our Lord would grant the prayers. She replied frankly, No. He told her to continue praying, and after awhile questioned her again. She then repeated to the Father word for word the five orders he had given her in his own mind, to his great astonishment. He saw that she must be led by the Spirit of God. However, without showing his surprise, he answered, " Speaking and action are two very different things. I will therefore put you to the proof later on as to whether you can really do what you say." She answered, that with the assistance of God and of the Blessed Virgin she was ready to obey, and to do all he had commanded; that to enable her to fulfil it she put her trust in holy obedience, in the will of God and of the Blessed Virgin. He then sent her away.

After some days he came back to the Convent, and ordered her to fulfil his first command. It was that the wound in her side should open. He ordered that it should take place whilst he said Mass, at which Mass Veronica was to assist. He offered the Holy Sacrifice, and after his thanksgiving, sent for Veronica to the confessional, and asked her if the wound was opened. She answered modestly, "Yes." "That is not enough," he replied; "put a piece of white linen on the wound, and then give it me." She did so, giving him the linen steeped in blood, and giving forth an agreeable odour. He then gave her the second command, forbidding the wound to close before his permission. She promised to obey, and the affair remained so for that day.

Crivelli wrote the Bishop a report of all that had taken place, sending him the linen with the blood on it, and smelling with odour, to the great astonishment of the prelate. An affair with the Grand Duke

of Tuscany, Como III., compelled Crivelli
to return to Florence, where he remained
twenty-two days. On his return to the
Convent he asked Veronica if the wound was
still open. On her answering it was, he
informed the Bishop that he might come and
see with his own eyes, and also be present at
the fulfilment of the third command. The
prelate presented himself, with the confessor,
at the grille of the choir. Veronica is
brought. Crevelli presents her with a pair of
scissors, and orders her, in virtue of holy
obedience, to cut her habit opposite to the
wound of the heart. She obeyed without
hesitation, and the Bishop, who had lighted a
candle to see better, beheld, as well as his
companion, that the wound was open and
bleeding. Crivelli, struck at the sight, said,
" Well, now I command that the wound close
up at once." Veronica remained some
minutes recollected in prayer, and on being
asked if the command were fulfilled, she
answered, " Yes." To assure themselves, the
two witnesses again looked through the cutting in the habit, which was moved aside,
and beheld the wound perfectly covered with
skin, like the other parts of the body. There

only remained a small scar. Stupified with amazement, they admired the works of the Lord. Father Ubald Cappelleti had, nine years before, made the same experiment with a like result.

There still remained the fourth and fifth commands to be fulfilled. One morning, then, about the middle of November, Veronica came of herself to the confessional, and said to Crivelli that she had learned that on the 29th, in the evening, the vigil of S. Andrew's feast, about nine o'clock at night, the sufferings of the Passion would commence, and so she would obey the fourth command, that her sufferings, with the dolours of our Blessed Lady, would continue for twenty-four hours: that nevertheless an order from him would at any moment cause the sufferings to cease. Crivelli, in doubt, said that he would see what should be done to fulfil the will of God. He then sent word to the Bishop of what Veronica had told him, and returned to his College.

But the following day, about five o'clock in the morning, word came in all haste from the Convent that Veronica was dying. Knowing already what was the matter, he

made no haste, but conferred on the subject
with the Rector of the College, Father Julio
de' Becchi. He received a second message,
and then went, with the Father Rector,
to the cell of Veronica, whom he found
dressed, but lying on her bed, under a covering of coarse wool, exhausted and scarcely
breathing. He made her recite the acts of
faith, hope, and charity, confessed her, and
then spoke to her of her interior state, which
had commenced at nine the evening before.
She had already suffered the agony in the
garden, the apprehension of our Saviour, His
presentation before Herod and Pilate, and
she was now given up to this act of the
Passion.

Crivelli saw by the light deeply imprinted
on her two hands the marks of cords that
bound the Saviour. Penetrated with that
feeling of terror which the supernatural ever
produces in us, he pointed these marks out
to the Rector and to some of the Nuns. He
then asked Veronica what was going to
follow. She replied, "The scourging." He
exhorted her to take courage, gave her abso-
lution again, and ordered her, in virtue of
holy obedience, to submit herself to this new

torture, but still, that when he commanded it should at once cease. The scourging then began, but to describe it best we cannot do better than cite the words of Crivelli himself.

"We saw her tormented in every sense on her bed, so that it was at the same time a spectacle admirable and horrible to see the violent movements of her body, which sometimes leapt into the air, and sometimes was cast with the head against the wall, and all this with such force that the boards of her bed were lifted up and fell back again. The walls of the cell were so shaken that it was like an earthquake. The Nuns ran in at the noise, fearing the roof was about to fall in on them, so that I was obliged to tell them to keep away. The Father Rector, seized with pity and dread, could support the spectacle no longer, and returned to the College without saying a word. After leaving her about an hour in this state, if I remember rightly, I put an end to it by saying, 'Enough; finish.' It was astonishing to see this woman, lost in contemplation of the mystery she suffered, and having no strength in her, all at once come completely to herself.

There she lay perfectly at peace, feeling nothing, and delivered from all her pains."

It was now ten or eleven o'clock when the scourging was over, and as Crivelli had not yet said Mass, he ordered Veronica, full of confidence in the virtue of obedience, to rise, and go to Choir to hear Mass. She rose at once and did so. When he had finished his Mass he told her to go back to bed. She went back to her cell, accompanied by the Abbess and some of the Nuns. He permitted her then to continue the mysteries of the Passion after the scourging. He soon saw signs of the crowning with thorns, then the carrying of the cross, and the walking to Calvary. These only appeared by the great sufferings they produced in her.

"Then," continues Crivelli, "came the crucifixion itself, and I may say that if I had seen her on a real cross the spectacle could not have been more rendered to the life. I had scarce given permission for the crucifixion, when her hands were stretched out so that the tension of all the muscles was quite apparent, and that the limbs were stretched to their very utmost extent. It was the same with the feet. Then her head bowed, and

she groaned most pitiably, her chest heaving
and falling violently. Her anguish just resembled that of a death agony. It was indeed
an agony; the death drops in cold sweat
poured from her forehead, tears bathed her
cheeks, and everything announced that she
was about to give up the ghost. She remained about half an hour in this state. She
seemed to be just about to breathe her last
breath when, full of faith through what I had
already seen, I ordered her to put a stop
to these sufferings. She did so, coming at
once to herself, and feeling nothing but a
great exhaustion."

Crivelli fortified her again by means of
spiritual remedies. She then recited the
office of the day with Sister Ceoli. And as
she remembered she had still to offer her
pains to the Blessed Virgin, he permitted her
to do so, adding that he would learn that she
did so by the beatings of her heart. Accordingly, the movements produced in her
heart by the pain she felt were so audible
that they were like the beatings of the pen-
dulum of a clock. "I then allowed her to
finish, and all ceased. About midnight I had
some food prepared for her, which I blessed,

She ate of this without that disgust which she ordinarily felt in taking food." Crivelli returned to his College, amazed at the wonders he had beheld. He sent an account to the Bishop, and begged him to fix a day for the execution of the fifth command. The Bishop fixed a day in the month of December.

When the day arrived, the Bishop and Crivelli went in the afternoon to the Convent of Veronica. They had the Church and Choir doors fastened. The Saint was behind the grate of communion, no one else being with her. Crivelli then ordered her, in the name of God, and by holy obedience, to suffer and to represent before the bishop the crucifixion upright on her feet. She prayed, therefore, a short while, considering the mystery she was about to reproduce in her person. Then says Crivelli, " Leaping up of a sudden, she stood on her feet, her arms stretched out violently in the form of a cross, so that her body seemed actually fastened to a cross. The motion and shaking were such that the seats of the Choir trembled, and the other Sisters, though at a distance, heard the noise quite distinctly. Seeing that amidst these movements, while the joints of her bones cracked, and the muscles of her arms were convulsed with cramps, yet she still was ever bounding about, I cried to her, ' Higher, higher.' Her body then mounted right into the air, so that her feet no longer touched the ground at all. Then she came down again. After remaining some time crucified thus, she suddenly cast herself all her length on her face on the pavement of the Choir, and remained some time in that position. I asked her afterwards why she fell in that position. She said it was to represent what the Jews did after they had nailed our Lord to the cross, turning the cross over to rivet the nails at the back. When this scene had lasted for about half an hour, we thought it time to stop. I gave Veronica the necessary permission, and it immediately ceased. She at once knelt down humble and recollected in our presence. The Bishop bade her farewell, and we left the church in astonished admiration at what we had beheld."

This clear and precise testimony of a man of irreproachable character, experienced, grave, clever, and prudent, confirmed too by a solemn oath, leaves no room for doubt or serious objection. Again, when what this man saw in Italy in his time has been seen at other times in Spain, France, Germany, and elsewhere, by witnesses just as unimpeachable, who can dare to attribute such phenomena to imposture, seeing nothing but a trick got up between those who produce them and those who witness them ? One must therefore make up one's mind to accept the physical and physiological facts as incontestable. All the question is, in what proportion to admit a superior influence in them. This influence may be, as has been seen in various cases, the intervention of the Saints. We shall cite, as an example of this, the case of Jane de Carniolo, named sometimes Jane d' Orvieto.

Having become an orphan at the age of three   **Jane de Carniolo.** years, a superior power seemed to take the charge of her. Some persons having asked the child one day who brought her into life, she led them into a church, before a statue of S. Michael, and said to them, " See, here is papa and, mamma." At the age of fourteen she entered the Third Order of S. Dominic, and arrived in a short while at a high degree

11

of sanctity. She suffered much injustice from
men, but she retaliated by acts of kindness,
insomuch that it was said of her at Orvieto,
" If you want Jane to pray for you, do her
some evil; you will soon experience the
effect of her prayers."

One Friday, when she was meditating on
the Passion of our Lord, the Sisters saw her
torn away by invisible hands, and her two
feet as it were nailed over one another. Her
face became blue and all disfigured. Her
bones were dislocated, the joints cracked;
and all, seized with dread, thought her about
to die. On the feasts of the martyrs she was
often ravished whilst considering in her
meditations the kinds of death they suffered.
She took the position in which they themselves had suffered, and endured in her body
the same tortures. On the Feast of S. Peter
the Apostle she was crucified like him. The
Sisters found her in extasy mid-air, her head
below, her arms extended, and her feet placed
one over the other. She was stiff and
motionless, as if really crucified with head
downwards, like the Apostle. The following
day, being the Commemoration of S. Paul,
they found her in extasy, kneeling with her

head bent, as if to receive on her neck the stroke of the axe of the executioner.

But if she took part in the sufferings of our Lord and of His Saints, she equally shared in their joys and triumphs. At Christmas the Infant Jesus appeared to her, and inundated her soul with a torrent of delights. They saw her on Ascension Day, contrary to the laws of gravity, lifted up in the air, radiant with delight, her hands joined and raised towards heaven, as if to mount with our Lord to His heavenly abode. She died in 1306. (Steill, July 23.)

CHAPTER VIII.

The Eye-witness of the Author himself.

MARIA MOERL.

TO facts of this kind, attested by grave and creditable witnesses, let it be permitted me to add here what I can bear testimony of for myself. I do not pretend to give my testimony as the guarantee of theirs, but because it does not seem suitable to speak of what has formerly happened of this nature, and leave untold events of the present day. It will be seen, moreover, by this, that the mysterious act of our Saviour's Passion is historic and universal, reproducing itself in all times, always the same, though taking in each individual case different forms and a different character.

I wish, then, to speak of Maria Moerl, of Calderno, in the south of the Tyrol. I will first try to show how this extraordinary state to which God raised her was developed in her, and then I will let the reader know how I found her myself, and what impression she made on me. What I relate about her life has been made known to me by persons worthy of credit, who were acquainted with her from her early years; Father Capistran, amongst others, her confessor, so conscientious in his declarations, that if he let slip even the smallest inexactitude he was careful to rectify it at once; M. Eberlé, Curé of the chief church of Botzen, and formerly pastor of Maria Moerl; Doctor Marchesani, of Botzen, who was her physician for a long time; M. Giovanelli, of Botzen, who knew her from

her infancy, himself being known in all the
Tyrol; Madame de Jasser, benefactress of the
family, whose testimony has quite as good
guarantees as those of the rest.

Maria de Moerl was born
October 16th, 1812. She was **Maria Moerl.**
brought up by her mother, a woman of piety
and good intelligence, and later on she helped
her with zeal and cleverness in the household
cares, which her circumstances had rendered
difficult. From her tenderest age she gave
evidence of excellent qualities. She was kind
to her school companions, sharing gladly with
them whatever she had, and rendering them
every service in her power. Without there
being anything remarkable in her, yet her
mind showed excellent dispositions; her
imagination was not over lively, nor did she
do anything to increase its being so. Then,
as later on, she read little; but she distinguished herself by intelligence and address,
by great benevolence towards the poor, and
by a great fervour in prayer, being very
devout in the church of the Franciscans,
which was close by her father's house.

She had very early to fight against the
evils of a sanguine constitution. When she

was but five years old, she lost a quantity
of blood coming from wounds in the stomach
or the bowels.   From that time she was very
often sick, and from an accident which happened to her when nine or ten years old, she
began to have frequent spittings of blood,
accompanied with great oppression on the
chest.   Then there came a dreadful pain in
the side, proceeding probably from an ob-
struction of the spleen.   This she has to this
day.   Spite of the cleverest doctors, this
disease has taken hold fast of her.   More
than once she has been ready to die, and
given over by the physician.   She got well,
however, but never has lost the germ of the
evil, and never has had sound health.   She,
however, became ever more serious and
pious, still more diligent at her exercises of
devotion.

From the age of thirteen years she had for
her confessor Father Capistran, a pious and
excellent priest, who has endured long sufferings.   He was at the same time the support
of the family, the faithful counsellor of her
mother, and their aid in all the difficulties
that a numerous family meets with when they
have not enough to keep them.   Maria being

now a little stronger, was sent over the mountain to Eles, to learn Italian. She remained there three quarters of a year, coming home only once to see her parents. When she took leave of her mother, whom she then saw for the last time, a piercing grief shot through her soul, as she herself declared later on, and she seemed to be unable to part from her. Then it was that that foreboding faculty of future events began to manifest itself, which later on declared itself in a more precise manner, when her mother actually died in 1827. Spite of the distance which separated them, it is said that Maria then knew the very hour of her mother's death. This circumstance, however, is not absolutely certain.

Maria's father was thus left a widower, with nine children, the youngest only ten days old. As he was not able to manage the house, this burden fell on Maria. She received it with joy, and executed her task with a clever zeal. But she became still more serious, more interior, more diligent at the church, and at her exercises of devotion, for she had much to endure, and had a heavy burden to carry. Her grief for her mother's loss was so deep, that after three years she was still seen to weep. Her regrets, however, were soothed somewhat when she had renounced all earthly things. Still her cares went on increasing day by day, and hard poverty, with the annoyances it brings in its train, pressed every day more hardly upon her. Her strength was not such as to be able to stand it long.

When she was eighteen she fell into a bad sickness; cramps of all kinds assaulted her already enfeebled body, convulsions agitated her limbs, and she lost quantities of blood. When the doctor came she had been nine-and-twenty days without any other food than a few spoonfuls of lemonade. He administered the remedies of his art, prescribed a regimen of diet, and she obtained a great relief. The cramps gradually ceased, and her constitution recovered from its exhausted state. Still there was no perfect cure; the pain in her side continued, and she became thinner and thinner every day. A year had gone by, when Maria asked the doctor if a cure was possible. He answered he could not promise a perfect cure, but only some relief of her pains. She replied with courage, that if she could not be cured she did not want the relief, and she was disposed to suffer all that God might send upon her. This resolution was probably inspired partly by a desire to abandon herself into the hands of Divine Providence, and partly by a wish to spare her father the expense of the purchase of remedies, so as not to augment his distress. What she asked happened. From that moment she suffered with an heroic resignation the great pains which never left her.

Such was her outward life. Now for her interior life, which is thought to be far less known. She had trials of various kinds, joined to the bodily pains she experienced, and, as is usual, temptations followed her in proportion as she advanced in those interior ways in which she was conducted by God. We shall speak further on about these temptations so singular. The frequentation of the sacraments was her only remedy against them.

From 1830 to 1832 she made in this manner rapid progress in the spiritual life, but nothing unusual was remarked in her. After 1832, however, her confessor perceived that sometimes she did not answer the questions he put to her, and that she appeared out of herself. He questioned those who were present with her, and was told that whenever she received Holy Communion she was out of herself. This answer struck him much. He had up to that time supposed, as others did, that what took place in her was the ordinary effect of her disease. For the first time he suspected there might be something more. He was confirmed in this thought when the phenomena in her took, later on, a more decided cast. At last a circumstance, which occurred this same year, gave him the key to these extraordinary states.

The procession of Corpus Christi was made at Calderno, as everywhere else, with great pomp. Cannon was fired, and the streets were filled with music. All this noise and motion passed through the windows of Maria. Noisy music always made a disagreeable impression on her, but the very sound of a violin, or of wind instruments, gave her a fit of violent cramps. Her confessor, busy with the preparations for the feast, wanted to have the day free, as also to spare her the

annoyance which all this tumult caused her.
And as he knew already that after Communion she remained six to eight hours in
extasy he thought it best to give her Communion in the morning, that she might be
at peace for the rest of the day. He accordingly brought the Blessed Sacrament to her
at three o'clock in the morning. He left her,
and was busy all the day. The next day he
was busy too, and he did not go to see her
till about three in the afternoon, when he
found her kneeling in just the same position
he had left her thirty-six hours before. Surprised, he questioned the people of the house,
and they told him she had been all the time
in extasy. In general they paid little attention to her in the house, leaving her to her
extasies and her prayers. When she wanted
anything she had to call some one for it.
Her confessor then understood how deeply
her being was penetrated with extatic influence, so that it had become to her a second
nature, and would become her habitual state
if some limit were not put to it. When he
recalled her to herself, he took upon himself
to regulate this state by the virtue of holy
obedience, of which she had made a vow

when received into the Third Order of S. Francis.

Her extasies had rendered the eyes of her soul very piercing. Several instances showed this. One day, being worse than usual, the sacraments were administered to her. A great number of people followed the priest into the room. Now on the table was a silver cup near her bed, into which the holy water had been put for the ceremony. Maria valued it much, either as given to her by her mother, or as a remembrance of some one. She received Communion, and fell into an extasy, as usual. When she came to herself the cup was missing. She was very grieved at its loss, and told her confessor. He comforted her as well as he could, and advised her to pray about it, and ask God to send it back again. She did so, and was successful. The first time she came out of her extasy she said, joyously, " I shall soon find my cup again." She was asked if she knew who had taken it. She said, " Yes; but I have prayed God to touch his heart, that he may give it back without having to blush for it." A week afterwards the cup was found in the kitchen amongst the other things. Another time she

warned some of those who were round her
to be careful of a certain board in her room,
because it was in danger of giving way. At
first they gave no heed to what she said, but
as she repeated the warning several times,
and always more and more urgently, they
had the plank looked to by some workmen,
and they found that the prop under it was
perfectly rotten, and that it threatened to
fall; the wonder was it had not given way
before.

Things were in this state when, in the
second half of the year 1833, a singular thing
occurred for Maria Moerl. The Tyrol had
soon learned of her extatic state. All at
once, and from all points at the same time,
a general movement took hold of the people.
Crowds arrived to behold with their own eyes
what they had heard of in legends, but had
never expected to behold in reality. Pro-
cessions from various parishes succeeded one
another without interruption, going to Calderno, preceded by the banner of the cross,
and the concourse was immense. From the
end of July to September 15th more than
forty thousand persons had visited the extatic, whose senses, open in appearance, were

really shut to the outer world, and whose
prayers and meditations were all within.
They wished to admire the spectacle, and
to be edified by its sight. No one could
explain all this concourse. The clergy, who
are afraid of such apparitions, and partly
with reason, were counted for nothing in
this matter. It seemed as though the same
Spirit that worked in the extatic moved and
pushed these masses to be witnesses of the
marvels He had wrought. Everything was
conducted in a very orderly way, and during
the seven weeks this concourse continued,
there was no excess to be deplored. Yet
there were days when the chamber of the
patient, which could contain at most fifty or
sixty at a time, was visited by three thousand.

The authorities, both spiritual and tem-
poral, desired to put a stop to these pilgrimages. The police were uneasy, as is
usual under such circumstances, and the
people were told that from this time forth no
more would be allowed to enter. The news
spread soon through the country, and the
pilgrimages ceased without discontent. But
the curés had long to bless God for the happy
effect the sight had had on their people. At

the end of the autumn of this year the prince-
bishop of Trent came to Calderno to take
information, and he heard various witnesses
on oath. The result was not published, nor
were the declarations of the witnesses, for
the affair was not yet ripe for a decided judgment. The bishop wished to have some
ground for giving an answer to the govern-
ment, which suspected these phenomena to
be superstition, or a pious fraud, or at least
some illusions proceeding from a too great
simplicity. The bishop then only declared
that the malady of Maria de Moerl did not
present in truth the characters of sanctity,
but that her real piety was not a disease.
The police after this was less annoying in its
measures.

The extatic herself never perceived all the
noise around her, except in the last times,
and then she was very much surprised at it.
Her interior spirit was matured in tran-
quillity, developing ever more and more.
The stigmata appeared on her body, and the
thing took place just as simply as with others.
Already in the autumn of 1833 her confessor
had remarked by accident that there was a
hollow in her hands, in the places where,

later on, the wounds appeared, as if there were some pressure on the parts. These parts were at the same time very painful, and had frequent cramps. Her confessor guessed that the stigmata were likely to make their appearance soon, and the event justified his expectations.

Two days after Candlemas in 1834, that is, February 4th, he found her with a piece of linen in her hands, with which she was wiping the blood from them, like a frightened child. When he saw the blood on the linen he asked what it meant. She answered that she did not know what had happened herself, that she must have cut herself somehow. But really it was the stigmata, which remained ever after on her hands, and soon began to appear on her feet. At the same time came the wound on her heart. Father Capistran acted most simply in the affair, not even asking her about her interior, to know what had given occasion for the appearance of the stigmata, so little pretension did he manifest for the marvellous.

The stigmata were about half an inch in diameter, and were round almost, but a little oval, and confined to the hands and feet.

On Thursday evening and Friday these
wounds often ran clear blood in drops. The
other days they appeared crusted with dried
blood, but there was no trace of ulceration,
nor of inflammation, nor any vestige of lymph.
She hid them, just as she kept secret all that
could manifest her interior. But in 1833, on
occasion of the solemn procession, an extatic
jubilation appeared in her. One day, in the
presence of several witnesses, she was surprised by an extasy, when she was seen like a
glorious Angel, scarce touching the bed with
her feet, radiant and beautiful, her arms
stretched out in the form of a cross, and she
plunged in the delights of heavenly love.
All present could then see the stigmata, so
that they were a secret no longer.

Her state was still miserable. In the
autumn of 1834 she was attacked with violent
and painful convulsions, which lasted several
weeks. Still, after Christmas, or rather
perhaps after the Feast of the Immaculate
Conception, she got back her freshness and
her good looks, and kept like this till the
end of the following summer. It was in the
autumn of this year that, when making a tour
in the south of the Tyrol, I saw her several

12

times. The situation of Calderno, her native place, is truly ravishing. On the right bank of the Etsch, from the mouth of the Eisach, rises a mountain of moderate height and graceful form, which runs over a space of eight or nine miles, and whose roots are mingled with those of another mountain chain, much loftier, which separates the valley of the Etsch from that of Nunsberg. Between these chains is a valley situated three or four hundred feet above the level of the Etsch, in the midst of which is a little lake clear and limpid, girt around with vineyards. There, on a gentle slope, rises Calderno, with its stone houses in antique style, circled by fresh landscapes, with villages, chateaux, and calvaries, with a far-stretching splendid view of the snow summits of the Alpine range on the one' side, and on the other side by bare or wooded peaks, which extend up the valley of the Etsch as far as Trent.

It is in one of these stone houses, of the fifteenth and sixteenth centuries, that Maria de Moerl lives. She sleeps in a little white-washed chamber, on a hard mattress, with linen always white and clean. Close by the bed is her little altar; at the back of it some pictures, to which she has a special devotion; they are attached to the window sidings, and there are venetian blinds to temper the vivid light, and cool the sultry air of this burning climate.

Maria de Moerl is of middle height, of delicate figure, as those of German descent usually are in the Tyrol; though the blood of so many different races is mingled with them, the Franco-Rhenish perhaps predominating. These people were probably brought hither by the Roman emperors, from the Rhine banks, to guard this important pass into the plains of Italy. For her food, Maria takes, from time to time, when she wants it, or her confessor tells her, a few grapes, or some other fruit, or a little bread; this is all. She has become exceedingly thin on this diet, but is not more so than many others who pursue an ordinary life. Her face indeed has a certain freshness, which, however, varies much according to her state of health.

The first time I visited her I found her in the position she usually takes, on her knees, at the edge of her bed, and in extasy. Her hands were crossed on her breast, so that one could see the stigmata. Her face, which was

turned upward somewhat, was directed towards the church. Her eyes lifted towards
heaven have such an absorbed look that
nothing outward could disturb. No movement was perceivable, except her breathing
and the swallowing of her spittle, unless just
the slightest wave of the body. She could be
compared only to an Angel prostrated in
prayer before the throne of God. No wonder
the sight of her produced such an impression
on those who were admitted to behold her.
The hardest hearts could not but be moved at
this spectacle. Joy, devotion, and amazement have caused many a tear to flow in her
presence.

For four years, according to the testimony
of her director and the curé, she has been
occupied, during her extasies, in contemplating the life and Passion of Jesus Christ,
and in adoring the Blessed Sacrament. Her
prayers follow the Church year. She has
written some out for her confessor, which,
according to his testimony, are full of fervour
and unction. The faculty of seeing things at
a distance, whether in time or space, is
exercised only in things that concern the
Church or God. It is very different from

that of somnambulists. She knows no more
than any other the things that take place in
her own body. The events she has foretold
were such that no foreboding could have
made known, but their accomplishment de-
pended on the ever-changeful will of man,
and on Divine Providence. Except to her
confessor, she has never spoken of her visions,
and how they blend with her life. But as her
knowledge is so limited, she feels a great
difficulty sometimes in finding words for what
she has seen. But the image seen by the
mind manifests itself clearly in the posture of
the body, which takes part more or less in
the vision. So at Christmas she seems to be
holding the new-born Infant in her arms,
nursing It with great joy. At the Epiphany
she is on her knees amongst the wise men.
At the marriage feast of Cana she is seen
reclining at table, after the eastern fashion.
This manner she cannot have learned from
pictures, because they do not so represent it.
On other days she equally represents in her
own person the subject on which she is
meditating.

But the object that most engrosses her mind
is the Passion of Christ. It is that which

makes within her the deepest impression, and shows itself most vividly without. In Holy Week it affects her in the most profound manner, and is most completely reproduced in her own person. Still every Friday of the year the contemplation of this mystery returns, so that there are frequent opportunities of beholding its marvellous effects. The simple and natural manner in which she goes through the representation of the great mystery is one of her most striking characteristics. For if we follow its every stage, from its first beginning to its completed climax, we shall find that each scene of the mighty drama is mingled with the impress of her own personality. It is seen that her mind has acquired the faculty, not merely of considering at a distance the object of her meditations, and so of just grazing it, so to speak : but the object becomes quite close to her ; she penetrates within it, she blends herself with it intimately ; it sways and masters her inmost life ; she leaves herself, and instead receives it, so as to become, in a sort, identified with it, one with it. Then the mind does with its object whatsoever it will. In proportion as this process of assimilation is developed, the reflected action appears in the body outside. The contemplation, thus clothed in a sensible form, becomes in its turn an object of contemplation also to the observer.

The drama is begun early on the morning of Friday, and as one follows it to its completion, one may see that, as many persons speak their thoughts, or think aloud, unconscious of the words they are uttering, so this extatic meditates on the Passion by reproducing it, or reproduces it in herself through her contemplation of it. The action is at first calm and regular; then by degrees, as it becomes more sorrowful and penetrating, the features of the picture which represents it show a more vivid likeness to it, and are more easily recognizable. When the hour of death comes, and the anguish has pierced to the very marrow of the soul, the woman becomes in every trait of her features the very image of death. There she is on her knees on her bed, her hands crossed on her breast. Around her is the stillest silence, broken hardly by the breathing of those present. You would say the sun of her life is setting, and in proportion as its light fades,

the shadows of death rise up from the abyss,
and veil successively each member of her
body under its darksome pall, the soul
struggling powerlessly against them till every
faintest ray is quenched.

Throughout the whole of the action she
was pale, but towards the close her pallor
much increased. The shudder of death runs
through her bones, and life hides more and
more under the thickening shadows. The
long heaving sighs from her breast show the
increasing oppression of her soul. From her
fixed eyes roll down slowly big tears over
her cheeks. Her mouth imperceptibly opens
wider and wider. As lightning before the
storm, so certain movements agitate her face
first, as it were, in small circles, then widen
over all its breadth, and at length shake the
entire frame from time to time with their
violence. The gentle sighs change into a
moan, which rends the heart to hear. A
deep flush clouds the cheeks, and the swollen
tongue seems to be glued to the parched
palate. The convulsions become ever more
violent and distressing. The hands began at
the outset to lose their power, and ended in
hanging lifeless. The nails turn blue, the

fingers clench convulsively, and the death rattle is heard in the throat. Her gasping breath struggles in the efforts of her stifled chest, which seems fast bound with bars of steel; her features become so disfigured as hardly to be known; her mouth opens to its fullest reach; her nose is pinched up; and her sunken eyes seemed to lose all power. At long intervals, however, still a sigh escapes from her stiffened form, till death comes; the last sigh goes forth, the head drops, the work of complete exhaustion of life is consummated, and there rests before us a face, a look, now unknowable.

It is only for two minutes or so she remains like this; then her face takes its old serene look, the head rises, the eyes are lifted up towards heaven, and she is occupied in presenting to God the homage of her gratitude. The same scene is renewed every week, but though it is the same in its principal features, there are always lesser variations, answering to the present peculiar dispositions of her soul. By an attentive watch I have ascertained this beyond doubt several times; for in this action there is no previous learning of a part; the whole flows naturally and without art from her inward self, as water wells from its spring. Nothing forced or exaggerated can be observed in the representation. Were she actually to die she would die just in this manner.

However absorbed Maria 'may be in contemplation, a single word from her confessor, or from any one else who has spiritual jurisdiction over her, is quite enough to bring her back to herself, and there is no perceptible transition to be remarked. She answers at once to the call, she just thinks, and opens her eyes, and in a moment all trace of extasy is gone. The first thing she does when waking, if people are present, is to cover her hands, as a child might hide her hands from her mother's eye when stained with ink. Being now accustomed to see strangers around her, she casts on them a sort of look of curiosity, and just gives each a friendly salute. She is not at her ease if she reads on the faces of the bystanders looks of admiring veneration, the result of the thrilling scenes they have witnessed, and by her playfulness she endeavours to blot out these deep impressions. As she does not now speak she tries to make herself understood by signs.

When she cannot succeed she looks at her confessor to help her, like a child unable yet to speak her first words. Her brown eyes have the simple look of a playful child. In their limpid transparency one can dip down to the innermost recesses of her soul. There are no dark corners there. Nothing like fraud could be there. There are no hiding places. All is simple; not the least trace of exaggeration or affectation; no false sentimentality, hypocrisy, or pride. She possesses the candour and innocent simplicity of childhood, which enjoys sportiveness, guarded by that delicacy of tact which instinctively avoids all unbecoming thought or expression.

When in the midst of her friends, she can, when out of her extatic state, remain so a considerable time; but one feels that for this she has to use strong efforts of her will. For extasy has become for her a second nature, and the ordinary state is to her an artificial one. In the midst of a lively conversation one may see her eyes grow heavy, and in a second, without any transition, she is in extasy. Whilst I was at Calderno she had been asked to hold at the font a new-born child. She took it in her arms with the most intense joy, and showed the greatest interest in the whole ceremony, yet she fell into extasy several times before its conclusion, and had each time to be recalled to herself.

The sight of these extasies is a most singular spectacle. She seems, as she lies back, to float in waves of light, and she casts around her a look of ineffable gladness. Then of a sudden she is seen, as it were, to enter deep into their abyss. Their billows play around her, and then cover her whole countenance with their transparent waters, so that it is enveloped in light. The simple child is now gone. Often in the very climax of her extasies her brown eyes are seen shining amidst her transfigured features. They are full open, but without being directed to any particular object. They seem to send their glances into the infinite. She is like the ideal of an inspired sybil, but of a dignity more noble still.

In giving herself to meditation and the exercise of devotion, we must not suppose her neglectful of the cares of the household. From her bed she directs all, a task formerly shared with her by a sister, now dead. By the interest of some kind souls she has had for some years a pension, but having no want for herself, she devotes it to the education of her brothers and sisters, whom she has placed, according to their dispositions, in various schools. At two in the afternoon every day she arranges affairs of business. Her confessor recalls her to herself, and she lays before him any difficulty, and gives orders. She manages everything, thinks of everything, and forestalls the wants of all who depend on her. She does all this with excellent common sense, and on this account all around her is always to be found in the very best order.

CHAPTER IX.

The Case of Domenica Lazzari.

[Added by the French Translator.]

IN a note to the work of Görres, in the German tongue, the author says that he will not speak of Domenica Lazzari, then living at Capriana, in another Alpine valley, because he had not seen her, and could not obtain information about her perfectly authentic. We shall supply this want, and fulfil his intentions, by transcribing for the reader a very interesting article in the *Université Catholique,* May, 1842, by Abbé Cazalès. Domenica is now dead, as also is Maria de Moerl; but a great number of our friends have visited both these persons at different times, and all they bear witness of is in perfect agreement, so that what is here related is as certain for us as if we had seen it ourselves.

Amongst those who from eye-witness have related these marvels may be cited Doctor Jarbe, one of the greatest professors of criminal law, whose premature death has been such a loss to his friends and to science. Then there is Dr. Phillips, Professor of Canon Law in the University of Vienna, whose name is a glory to science and to the Church. There is also Guido Görres, who so nobly continued the glory of the name of his father, but died in the flower of his age.

Domenica Lazzari. The Abbé Cazalès, having spoken in the first part of his article of Maria de Moerl, whom he had himself visited, then continues in these terms: "To the description just given I will add some details about Domenica Lazzari, drawn from various sources. The most important are from a medical journal published at Milan, in which Dr. Leonard dei Cloche describes at great length the different states in which he has found this extraordinary person.

Domenica, youngest daughter of Lazzari the miller, was born at Capriana, March 16, 1815. Educated according to her condition, she early gave tokens of her intelligence and piety. During the intervals of work she liked to read books of devotion, especially those of S. Liguori. She prayed and meditated frequently, but was so reserved that no mark of extraordinary fervour escaped her. She only appeared a pious and virtuous girl. She enjoyed good health till her father's death in 1828, but her grief was then so excessive that it brought on a long sickness. However, she got well of this at last, either through medical treatment, or through the healing force of nature. But on June 10, 1833, says Dr. dei Cloche, whilst she was at work in the fields, a strange, painful feeling seized her of a sudden, and kept her pinned to the spot, unable to move, though at no great distance from the house. Those who happened to be near saw her standing as if lost in contemplation, or in extasy. She had a nervous attack for about an hour, during which, as she explained later on, she suffered a burning thirst, a very great difficulty of breathing, and she saw at a certain distance from her a venerable looking man, who told her to stand still while he should communicate to her something of importance.

When she came to herself the vision disappeared, and she was with great difficulty brought into the house. The following day she was seized with a malady of which the symptoms were first a continual cough, a feeling of choking, and cruel pains in the lower part of the belly. Later on other symptoms were added, and she was so ill she could not leave her bed. In the beginning of April, 1834, she felt such an aversion for all sorts of food or drink that she refused even the small amount she had been accustomed to take. At the end of the month she was pressed so to take something that for the last time she ate a little bread soaked in water.

On the 30th of April her parents, alarmed
by the violence and obstinacy of the malady,
went to Cavalèse for Dr. dei Cloche, who
describes the state he then found her in, and
the violent convulsions she had in his presence. He made various attempts to get her
to swallow some medicine, but having found
she could not possibly swallow anything, he
was obliged to give up any endeavour of
medical treatment. On August 29, 1834, he
came to see her again. He found her convulsions, instead of being periodical, had
become continual, but were less violent. Her
senses became all so preternaturally acute
that she could not bear the least light, nor
noise, nor smell. Any of these caused her to
have a fit of sobbing, with groans and convulsive movements. She could scarce articulate in a hoarse voice any single word. If
any one went near her bed by curiosity,
without great precaution, it caused her pains
and convulsions to increase. She had taken
no food, and all secretions were suspended.

The account given in the annals of universal medicine gives no particulars as to
how Domenica passed from the state here
described to that in which she is at the

13

present time. Doctor dei Cloche had quitted
Cavalèse, and had gone to Trent, as director
of the civil and military hospital. But three
years after, having heard of the strange
phenomena that had rendered the name of
the peasant girl of Capriana famous, he wished
to go himself and see what it was, and accordingly arrived for his visit, Thursday,
May 4, 1837, at four o'clock in the afternoon.

"She was lying in the same bed," he says,
"wrapped up with the same linen bandages,
and placed in the same posture as I had seen
her in August, 1834. Her hands were joined,
or rather clasped together, in the position of
prayer. On her forehead, two fingers' breadth
beneath the roots of the hair, from one temple
to the other, was a line of points pretty near
to one another, on which fresh blood was
shining. There were ten or a dozen of these
points. The rest of her face, as far as the
upper lip, was covered with dry blackish
blood. On the outside of the hands, about
the middle, that is, above the middle and the
ring finger, there rose a black spot, like
the head of a thick nail, perfectly round,
and about an inch in diameter. The centre
was raised higher than the sides, and looked

at in the light it had the appearance of clotted
blood dried. Round these spots were smaller
lines of scars, all verging to this centre.
Their colour was a pale brown, and they were
a quarter of an inch long. On the top of the
right foot, about the centre, was a mark like
those of the hands, with several lines round
it, like rays parting from the centre. I could
not see the top of the left foot, for it was
jammed close to the right, and wholly covered
by the sole of the right foot. Domenica
speaks slowly, her voice was plaintive, her
words full of life and energy. Her mind
appeared calm; her body was ever in a tremble, like a leaf agitated by the wind. When
I was close to her bed she gave me a smile of
welcome, and told me how glad she was to
see me. I told her how I compassionated her
state. She made no answer, but lifted her
eyes to heaven, and bowed her head. I asked
her several questions, so as to ascertain what
she suffered within. She answered these with
a good grace. Having asked to see the
palms of her hands and the soles of her feet,
which were almost horizontal as compared
with that of her legs, she replied, ' I cannot
move; it is at present impossible for me

to separate one hand from the other, or
one foot from the other foot. The smallest
effort I might make to satisfy you would
cause me horrible pains and frightful convulsions.'

"My curiosity was not content with this
excuse; I renewed and pressed my request,
and strove to find good reasons to persuade
her. She kept silent a few moments, and
then said, 'To-morrow morning I will try to
satisfy your desire, and I hope to be able
to succeed.' 'At present,' I said, in my
turn, 'if you have not the force to separate
the hands, try at least to move the fingers.'
She answered she could only move the fore-
finger of the right hand. I then asked her if,
on the morrow, which was a Friday, the
blood would flow from her body as on the
Fridays past. She answered, 'Up to this
present time I have never missed this martyrdom. My wounds have always bled on
that day. To-morrow morning, when I have
meditated the holy Mass, come and see me,
and you will be convinced of the truth. If
you come before your visit will distract me
from my prayers, and will be troublesome
to me.' I asked permission to feel her pulse,

and she consented; but she added, 'Do not press my arm too hard, for fear it should bring on long and violent convulsions. This happened only lately when a doctor, not believing in my sufferings, would feel my pulse in spite of me.' I did as she desired, but I could not discern any pulsation at all, for her body was in a continual tremble, and this prevented my feeling it. Though I touched her but lightly, my touch made her body tremble still more, and her groans redoubled.

"I asked her why her window was always open. She answered, 'Since the beginning of my sickness I cannot bear it shut, either day or night, even the coldest nights of winter. When any one has shut it, it has been forced to be re-opened, for fear of my being suffocated.' What she told me was attested to me by unimpeachable witnesses. It is notorious that during the winter of 1836, when the thermometer was down thirteen degrees below zero Réaumur, her window remained always open. She declared that when there are storms of wind she feels better, and her pains are relieved. She begs those who visit her to fan her; there is a large fan for this purpose. To verify her statement, I took the fan, and fanned her with all my force, sending her hair flying about her face. She liked this, and with her mouth half open she received the bluster of the fan, which to any one else would have been very disagreeable. She assured me she had a great wound in her side, which she kept carefully concealed, and other small ones along the spine, which all bled on Fridays. She added she had not slept, nor eaten a morsel, nor drunk a drop of water, since May 2, 1834. She said she suffered a continual martyrdom in her whole body, but particularly in the wounds; that her pains on Fridays had added to them palpitations of the heart, and were so intolerable sometimes that death would be a boon.

" Next day, May 5, I went at 7 a.m. to see Domenica. A hundred yards from the house I heard, from her window looking into the street, piercing cries, and on getting nearer could distinguish the words, 'My God, help me.' When I stepped into the room the most heart-rending spectacle met my eyes. The spots in the middle of the hands were now hollow wounds flowing with blood.

Blood ran also from both the wounds of the feet. Round each wound was a reddish glow, small round the wounds in the forehead. That of the other wounds resembled what is seen in vaccination on the seventh day of its development. These open wounds were like deep red raw ulcers, without any matter, or anything tending to corruption. The blood that came out was ruddy and tenacious, like artery blood. It flowed slowly, but quite visibly. The wounds of the forehead were a quarter inch deep, and an eighth of an inch wide. The wounds of the hands and feet were half an inch in diameter, and three-eighths of an inch deep, in the form of a cone. Having looked at Domenica awhile, I reminded her of her promise to let me see the palms of her hands. She at once raised her joined hands with a sigh, and detached them from each other. I saw only a surface wound all bleeding. She was unable to detach the right foot from above the left. As I desired to see the wound in the side, she said she could not let it be seen, because her chemise stuck to it, and could not be removed without insufferable pain whilst it bled, and when not bleeding the clotted blood com-

pletely hid it. This wound has only by
stealth been seen by her mother and sisters
whilst assisting her in her most violent convulsions. No one has seen those along the
back.

"At ten o'clock in the morning Domenica
was still crying out at the top of her voice,
'O my God, help me.' She just gave short
answers at intervals to the questions addressed
to her, and then continued her exclamations.
At four o'clock in the afternoon the blood
had ceased to flow, but she still continued
her cries of anguish. Being asked the reason,
she replied, 'I feel frightful pains in every
part of my body, and crying out relieves me a
little.' A little after she said, 'O my God,
I feel the pains in my chest;' and she made
signs with her hands that the pain had got to
the heart. 'It is,' she said, 'the signal
forerunning my worst sufferings.' Indeed,
ten minutes after she had a fit of the most
horrible and strange convulsions, extremely
violent. These dreadful spasms attacked her
without order or measure in every part of her
body, first one and then another. Their
mode was so various and capricious that it
would be impossible to describe them. She

was reduced so low by them that she seemed like death personified. What she experienced had no sort of relation either with her usual pains, her constant fasts, the continual bleedings each week, nor her frail constitution.

"To give a description, in all their forms, of the attacks to which Domenica is subject, it must be said that she is subject to every kind of convulsion, tonic and chronic, in turn; S. Vitus' dance, tetanus partial and general, convulsive suffocation, cynic spasms, trisumus, a sort of carpbology, and other affections of the same nature. Spasmodic paroxysms presented themselves under such various and capricious forms as to remind the observer of the words of Sydenham: 'Tam diversa sunt symptomata, atque ab invicem contraria, specie variantia, quam nec Proteus lusit unquam, nec coloratus spectatur chameleon.' Let me observe, lastly, that during her convulsions Domenica gave her chest blows with her joined hands so violent as to make a tremendous noise; and the grinding of her teeth could only be compared to that of a famished dog crunching bones, or the sound of a large file filing an iron bar.

"I shall, in conclusion, relate certain circumstances of the malady, which have been told me by persons worthy of credit. On May 12, 1836, she had a lipothymy, which lasted till the 16th of the same month. The only sign she gave of life was just the smallest movement observable. The strongest convulsions she had took place on June 24, 1836, and they continued without intermission to the evening of July 2. The strokes she gave herself with her joined hands were so loud as to be heard distinctly in the street four perches distant. There were counted four hundred and nine blows in an hour."

The above description gives as much details as one could wish for of the outward phenomena experienced by Domenica Lazzari. Her inward state is as little known as that of Maria de Moerl, because their directors have observed that discreet reserve that is prescribed in all such matters by the Church. Maria de Moerl was, with rare exceptions, in a state of continual extasy. Domenica Lazzari, on the contrary, had the use of her senses, unless at periods of less or greater length, when she betrays scarce any sign of life. These two cases, then, differ exceedingly. Domenica, who can take no food, can still receive Communion, and it is said she tells her confessor on what days to bring her the Holy Eucharist, which is ordinarily consumed without difficulty. However, on August 2, 1838, after receiving the sacred Host she was immediately seized with violent convulsions, which prevented her swallowing the species. This state lasting several hours, an attempt was made to withdraw the Host, but in vain, for whenever the endeavour was made the convulsions became so violent that nothing could be done. The sacred Host therefore remained on her tongue for two months, she not being able to consume it, and the attempt to withdraw it always failing. On September 24th she was able to swallow it. During all the interval she was, so to speak, like a living tabernacle.

CHAPTER X.

The Case of Louisa Lateau.

(Added by the English Translator, from the work of Dr. Lefebvre.)

THE latest famous example of the stigmata is that of Louisa Lateau. At the outskirts of the village of Bois d'Haine, situated between Mons and Charleroi, in Belgium, in the midst of a rich and prosperous country, may be seen by the roadside, in a rustic and retired spot, a lowly cottage. Its clean whitewashed walls, set off by green shutters and a red-tiled roof, give it, however, a fresh and agreeable look. Here was born, January 30, 1850, Louisa Lateau, third daughter of Gregory and Adela Lateau. Her father, a short, thick-set man, gained his living in an iron foundry. When Louisa was but three months old her father died of a virulent attack of small pox.

When Louisa was eight years old she was sent to tend an old woman, bed-ridden and helpless, during several months, and when

eleven she went to service with her great
aunt at Manage, who was in easy circumstances. She was afterwards in service at
several other places, in all of which she kept
the same good character, and became much
beloved. But her mother wishing her to be
at home, she returned, and helped in sewing,
and in the general labours of the house.

In 1866 the cholera ravaged Belgium, and
appeared at Bois d'Haine. Louisa helped the
priest of the parish, and nursed the sick,
going from house to house. She was after
this herself very ill with angina of the
pharynx, and she suffered much from neu-
ralgia. In 1868 she became so weak that
she received the last sacraments. It was
about a week after this, April 24, on a
Friday, that she first noticed some blood
coming from her side. She did not speak
of it; but the next Friday the same thing
occurred, and blood flowed also from the
surface of each foot. She now mentioned it
to the priest, who bade her say nothing about
it; but the next Friday, May 8, the blood
flowed during the night from the two feet
and the side, and also from the two hands,
both the backs and the palms. It could not

be kept secret any longer, and the priest told her to consult a doctor about it.

From this date every Friday the blood flowed, and finally, on September 25th the blood came from various points in the head. The first symptoms of the bleeding are seen ordinarily on Thursday about noon. There appears a sort of blister on the hands and feet, which gradually rises, filled with watery matter. This watery fluid sometimes takes a. reddish tinge, because the skin, being tough, it does not break before the blood mingles somewhat with the watery matter. The flow of the blood commences ordinarily during Thursday night, or early on the Friday morning, before 1 a.m. The stigmata do not all begin to bleed together, but sometimes one, sometimes another, begins first. Oftenest that in the side begins the first.

The way it takes place is as follows. The blister fills with matter, then bursts so as to let the matter escape, and then, the cutis or under skin being laid bare, blood begins to flow from its surface. Sometimes the skin of the blister is carried away with the rush of blood, leaving the wound bare; but sometimes, especially with the palms of the hands and the soles of the feet, the skin is so tough that the blood is retained by it, and clots there. The blood from the side flows from between the fifth and sixth ribs, slightly below the middle of the left breast. At first the blood flowed from three minute wounds without blister, but afterwards a blister formed, as on the hands and feet, and on its breaking the blood flowed from the under skin from a circular spot, about half an inch in diameter.

The bleeding of the head is more difficult to examine, because of the hair being matted and filled with blood, but on the forehead the task is easy enough. Here there was no trace of blister. The blood issued from twelve or fifteen minute points. When examined by a magnifying glass the blood is seen to flow through tiny scratches in the outer skin of various forms. The circle of these wounds is midway between the roots of the hair and the eyebrows. A band of an inch and a half would cover them all if passed round the head.

The quantity of blood lost by Louisa varies considerably. During the first few months after the stigmata showed themselves, the

flow was much more abundant than it is now
and was estimated by the first witnesses at
nearly thirty ounces. Dr. Lefebvre . estimated the quantity later on at full eight
ounces. Twice it altogether failed. On the
first occasion the stigmata remained entirely
dry, and on the second blisters formed, and
some matter flowed, slightly tinged with
blood. These have been the only two exceptions. The blood is of a light purple colour,
not red, like artery blood, nor of the darker
tint of venous blood ; it is, in fact, the blood
of the capillary veins. The flow of blood
comes at no fixed hour. The next day,
Saturday, the stigmata are dry. They then
present the following appearances. On the
back and palm of each hand there is an oval-
shaped surface, about an inch long, which
has a smooth glazed look, but is not moist.
The shape on the instep of the feet is an
oblong square, with the angles rounded off,
and the length is about an inch.

The stigmata are evidently the seat of
considerable pain, which is shown on the
features of Louisa. But except on Fridays
she works at the ordinary labours of the
house, and goes each day to hear Mass,

at the church, which is a walk of more than half a mile from the house.

The weekly extasies of Louisa began on Friday, July 17, thirteen weeks after the appearance of the stigmata. The extasy is renewed every Friday, beginning at eight or nine o'clock in the morning, and lasting till six or seven in the evening, a period of nine to eleven hours. It generally comes upon her in prayer. She is seated in a small cane arm-chair, with her bleeding hands clasped together, and wrapped in a cloth. She says her Rosary, and her whole countenance marks the repose of her soul. Suddenly her eyes become riveted and immoveable; they are raised towards heaven, and the extasy is commenced. Sometimes she falls into the extasy whilst in conversation. Dr. Lefebvre says: "I copy from my notes. It is half-past seven. I am talking with the young girl. I question her upon her work, her progress in instruction, her health. She answers these questions in a simple, precise, laconic manner. Her whole look is calm, the expression of her face natural. The conversation flags, there is a pause. I speak again, but perceive that Louisa does not move; her

14

eyes are raised up. She is in extasy. In order to impede the extasy, she was ordered by a Religious, who was appointed to watch the theological aspect of the case, to work at a sewing machine on Friday. She did as she was bidden, the blood flowing profusely from her hands and feet and from her fore-head. While Bishop d'Herbomez was questioning her, the noise of the machine suddenly ceased, and she was seen to be in extasy."

During her extasies Louisa for the most part remains seated, her body slightly bent forward towards the edge of her chair. She is motionless as a statue. Her bleeding hands, hidden from sight in their covering, rest on her lap, while her eyes, full open, are raised upwards. Her whole attitude is that of one absorbed in contemplation of some distant object. Her posture and her expression, however, vary much, and sometimes the eyes soften, and the lips are parted with a beatific smile. Then again a look of pain harrows the countenance, and the tears run down her cheeks; or at times there is seen a. terror-stricken gaze, accompanied by starts and stifled cries. She does not always sit: sometimes she rises and comes forward, standing on tiptoe, in an eager, expectant attitude, as if about to take flight. The hands are uplifted, clasped, or spread wide open in the position of the Orantes in the catacombs. The lips move, and the countenance has on it a halo of glorious beauty, as that of an angelic being. Add to this the terrible spectacle of the brow crowned with its bleeding diadem, the crimson drops trickling down over the cheeks. Who of the groups of men and women that surround her can remain unmoved by deep, awe-struck emotion?

At about half-past one in the day the extatic falls on her knees, her hands joined, her body bent forward, as in deep contemplation. After half an hour she rises and reseats herself. About two it is she rises suddenly, and falls with her face to the ground. Her feet are stretched out, but covered by her dress, and her head rests on her left arm. At three she throws out her arms in the form of a cross, and her two feet place themselves, the sole of the left on the upper surface of the right. In this position she remains till five, when she rises with a sudden bound, falls on her knees for a few

14 *

minutes, and then sits down again. The extasy terminates in a most appalling manner; the head droops on the chest, the eyes close, the nose becomes pinched, the face deadly pale, and covered with a cold sweat, and the death rattle is heard in her throat. This state lasts ten or fifteen minutes, then the eyelids fall, the features relax, the eyes look about on the surrounding objects,—the extasy is over. Louisa, having been questioned as to what takes place during these extasies, says that various scenes of the Passion pass before her. She remembers all, but will only speak when compelled by obedience.

No one that has known Louisa Lateau suspects her of fraud for a moment. But strangers to her life are naturally more suspicious. She has been put amply to the test by both friends and foes, and here some of the tests will be related.

Dr. Lefebvre, on Friday, February 11, 1870, having previously announced that he should not come on that day, as he had an engagement at a distance, and that no one was to be admitted in his absence, was unexpectedly called professionally into the immediate neighbourhood. He thought the opportunity

was therefore not to be lost of visiting Louisa.
He knocked at the cottage door, and passed
at once, when it was opened, to the apart-
ment of Louisa. It was about a quarter
to four. There she lay prostrate on the
ground. The blood flowing from the forehead had dried on the face; that from the
left hand was still flowing; the blood from
the right had ceased, but what had come was
still wet; the feet had not bled that day. He
left the cottage without Louisa knowing of
his entry or departure, she being all the
while in her extasy.

Some persons suspected that the blisters
of the stigmata were artificially raised by
means of caustics, such as cantharides or
ammonia. Now, first it must be remarked
that in case of a blister thus raised, the cutis,
or under skin, thus laid bare, never bleeds.
To put this objection to silence, Dr. Lefebvre, in the presence of two eminent
medical men, poured on the back of the left
hand, close by the stigma, some liquid
ammonia, which raised a blister the size of a
sixpence. In twelve minutes the blister had
filled with matter. It did not burst of itself,
so the doctor removed the epidermis, or outer

skin, leaving the under skin bare. The two wounds were therefore side by side, having precisely the same conditions; but whilst the real stigma flowed plentifully with blood, the stigma thus artificially made did not yield a single drop.

Another trial was the *glove test*, which has been described in a former case, and which was applied with the most careful precautions, and it was found the bleeding continued, though no access could be had to the parts affected.

Another test was her insensibility to pain. The skin was tickled with a quill in the parts most susceptible to the touch, the inner part of the nostrils and ears, but with no effect. Strong liquid ammonia was placed underneath the nostrils, but no notice was excited. Dr. Lefebvre, folding the skin of the fore arm, pierced it through and through with a pin. He plunged a penknife sharply into her arm, and remaining perfectly still for a few minutes behind her chair, suddenly pierced the nape of the neck, so that the blood spurted out in a stream; the result was always the same. None of the doctors present could perceive the slightest trace of sensibility. The last

experiment of this nature was one with a
strong electro-magnetic battery. It is well
known that a strong shock produces intolerable pain if continued for five or six
seconds; but here, though applied to the
tenderest parts for more than a minute at
a time, the features did not move in the
slightest, but preserved throughout their look
of deep, extraordinary, calm repose.

An experiment of a different kind was tried
on the young girl by Bishop d'Herbomez,
Bishop of British Columbia. The curé of the
parish, M. Abbé Niels, had returned from
communicating a sick woman, and entered,
with the Bishop, the chamber of Louisa. As
Louisa recognizes with a smile objects which
have received the Church's blessing, such
as medals and scapulars, it occurred to the
bishop to see what effect the holy oils would
have if brought near to her. Now in the
country parts of France the pyx and the
holy oils are often kept in two silver
vessels attached to each other, but still
separable from each other. As there had
been only one particle in the pyx, with
which the curé had communicated the sick
woman, the pyx was thought to be quite

empty. Now they wondered in what way she would recognize the presence of the holy oils, so the Abbé Mortier approached Louisa, intending to apply the silk bag in which the vessels were contained to her lips. But when about two yards distance from her, she started, trembling violently, and seeming to thrill with a transport of joy. Rising from her chair, she fell upon her knees in adoration, her whole expression being fired with divine love. As the Abbé drew back, she half rose and followed, gliding after him. If he paused she again fell on her knees. It struck him that a fragment of the Host must be still in the pyx, undiscovered by the curé. Accordingly, the vessel of the holy oils was separated by them from the pyx, and brought to her. When he touched her lips with it she simply smiled, as was usual when other blessed objects were presented to her. But when the pyx was again brought to her within a distance of two yards, the same scene of rapt adoration was renewed. On leaving the cottage, the bishop, the curé, and two others, went to the church, and on examining the pyx a considerable fragment of the sacred species was found to have remained in the case. Later on, to prove that there was no illusion, or mere clairvoyancy in this adoration, a silver case like the pyx, with an unconsecrated host, and contained in the silken bag as before, was presented by the curé before Louisa, but she remained quite motionless, taking no notice at all of it.

Louisa is still alive; she is still with her sisters. Since the Feast of the Epiphany, 1879, she remains lying on her bed. She for three years neither eats, nor drinks, nor sleeps. She communicates every day at half-past six o'clock in the morning; devout women are allowed to be present at the time of her communion on Fridays. Visitors come almost every day. The stigmata are as described above. On Fridays, from two to three o'clock, such men are admitted as have procured the requisite permission from the ecclesiastical authorities.

Richardson and Son, Printers, Derby.